Bean Hive Cottage I Smell Fall

Lucille Huckelbarel

Epilogue

Epilogue

"The best conversations start with coffee and end with 'You have to read this.'"

— Bean Hive Cottage

Dedication

To the dreamers, the doers,
and the caffeine-dependent thinkers.
To the moms who talk fast,
and the daughters who listen (mostly).
To the friends who become family
over endless cups of coffee and laughter echoing through old café
walls.
And to every cozy town where fall feels like magic,
and life smells just a little like cinnamon and possibility.
*Here's to good books, good banter, and the kind of love that feels like
home.*

Introduction

WELCOME TO BEAN HIVE COTTAGE

Bean Hive Cottage:

© 2025 Lucille Huckelbarel

Hello, I'm Lucille Huckelbarel, I'm glad you stopped by to-day-where witty humor exists. You have found your way to this comforting whimsical space of laughter and delight. Some would consider a visit to Bean Hive Cottage as "Therapy."

Open the book, grab a brew, and embrace this special community that has been stitched together of friendship, imagination, love, books and coffee. Bean Hive Cottage was created as a reminder that comfort can exist in simplest forms; a warm mug, a smile, story time, the Bean Hive Cottage Book Club. Yes, that is where it all began, in a world that rushes our thoughts, minds, time, "STOP!" Come savor life's moments of funny, messy, unexpected, perfectly imperfect.

Bean Hive Cottage was born from a longing for connection in a world that often forgets to slow down. People are either chasing after something, running away from something, hiding something, missing something, or simply not happy nor satisfied. I wanted to create the ultimate "EXPERIENCE" of feeling like you belong somewhere.

The stories here aren't just about cinnamon rolls, fall festivals, or eccentric neighbors-they're about the courage to show up and belong. Between these pages you will meet the most incredible, interesting, messy, and marvelous characters. You will take a breath and feel a bit more human, you will laugh with chills and know that you will always belong at Bean Hive Cottage. Please check us out online, we actually have "VIRTUAL BOOK CLUBS" that is right! Please check us out to see when the next one is happening. Join the club.

Bean Hive Cottage books are more than just books. Bean Hive Cottage books are filled with connection to the characters, and the love of amazing, interesting stories. Bean Hive Cottage Newsletter, please join online to access the most current happenings. That's right, you get to experience your very own Bean Hive Cottage experience, not just with books, but a book club. So stay as long as you would like, read with your heart open, laugh out loud, and know that you always have a seat waiting for you here-at the corner table of Bean Hive Cottage.

Warm mugs and cozy hugs,
Lucille Huckelbarel

Contents

Chapter 1

I SMELL FALL

Leaves, lattes, and a whiff of chaos. Lucy burst into Marvin's Diner, bundled in a fluffy scarf despite it being a balmy 67 degrees, and declared, " I smell fall! It's in the air-the pumpkins, the apples-the whole glorious, crunchy spectacle. I can practically hear the leaves shouting, 'Free at Last!' as they blow down Maple Street.

Marvin rolled his eyes over the rim of the coffee pot. "You smell Floyd Picklewitz's pumpkin spice cologne. He just started marketing it as 'Autumn Essence for the Everyday Man.' The Everyday Man is currently giving my regulars watery eyes."

Lucy, still in the doorway like a caffeine fueled windstorm, blinked, "What is Floyd Picklewitz's up to now-wait, he's got a cologne? Pumpkin spice, but make it wearable?"

"Yup," Marvin said. "It's his new line at the apothecary. He thought Autumn Essence for the Everyday Man would be appealing. The label has a squirrel in a top hat."

Lucy grinned. "I don't know which is more appealing -the word 'Autumn' for marketing, or the fact that he's leaning hard into the Fall Festival buzz. Perhaps he could rent a booth with a banner that reads, 'Autumn Essence for the Everyday Man -stop by and have a slice of fall.' Free sniff with purchase ."

The morning crowd turned to look as if fall itself had waltzed in and ordered a maple latte. Lucy clasped her hands. "I'm very excited for the village scarecrow contest, and I'm counting down to the big Fall Festival."

Marvin gave her a look that was half warning, half amusement. "You walked in carrying autumn."

Right on cue, Floyd Picklewitz materialized, gleaming with civic pride and nutmeg. "She calls it decor," Marvin said. "I call it a health violation,"

Lucy held up the leaf strewn basket. "What are you going to do, Marvin? You can't-take- fall out. Also, you already have beautiful decorations -thanks to me." The diner laughed; even the pie case seemed to smile.

"Anyway Marvin said, surrendering to the season, "the mayor's got the sign up sheet for the annual Fall Festival over at Town Hall. The baker, the dance studio, the apothecary, and the candy shop already signed up,"

"Fantastic!" Lucy said. " I need to get there and claim a booth. And I hope Squire the Squirrel is still the mascot. I felt terrible about last year -when that rogue acorn fell during the windstorm and bonked him like a cartoon. I was literally cutting onions all day. I don't think I ever cried so much in my life, for such a small critter of big importance. Afterall it's not everyday that a squirrel is a mascot."

Marvin nodded. "He's fine now. Took a little recovery time, but he's back to his mischievous self -climbing windows, zipping up trees, stopping traffic with interpretive tail flicks. Squire is festive already."

Lucy lit up. " Perfect. It's like Groundhog's Day- but with more personality. Do they rotate groundhogs? I mean, if Squire needed a break, we could have a substitute squirrel. There's a union for that, right?

"Wouldn't know about groundhogs," Marvin replied. "But for our Fall Festival, we have a mascot, and it's a squirrel. It's always been a squirrel.

Floyd, never one to let a gathering go unnoticed, clapped his hands. "Excellent news about the scarecrow contest! And the pie throwing contest! And the hot dog eating contest! It will be spectacular." He paused grandly. "However -might I suggest we consider the mascot? Squirrels are small, and puny, even.

Lucy frowned. "That's not kind. We've always had a squirrel. If not a squirrel, then what?"

Marvin shrugged. "Maybe a bear?"

Lucy stared. "A bear. For a village festival. Yes, nothing says family fun like 'Do not feed the mascot."

Floyd sniffed his own wrist, apparently moved by his product. "I propose a vote! Perhaps this is the year we embrace change. Progress smells like cinnamon."

Lucy turned to the room. "No one wants a bear, right?" The diner went respectfully silent -the kind of silence that says we are not voting for a bear because we enjoy having garbage cans that remain upright.

She smiled, triumphant. "See? Squirrel it is. We'll have the scarecrow contest, the pie throwing contest, the hot dog eating contest, and the squirrel mascot. Tradition with a dash of chaos -just how fall likes it."

Marvin slid a steaming mug of espresso Lucy's way, and winked at her. "Fine. But you can't bring that basket with dirty leaves into my nice, clean diner."

Lucy inhaled the coffee like it was legal sunshine. "Oh Marvin. I didn't bring the leaves in." She gestured to the window, where a wind gust swirled orange, gold and red foliage. "Autumn confetti, caffeine bliss, the town is covered in autumn confetti while life gets deliciously complicated."

Marvin grins. "Falling leaves, rising coffee orders, -just another day in paradise."

Lucy laughs and grabs a red leaf out of her basket. "Every leaf is a story, and this one begins with coffee."

Marvin grabs his kitchen towel to wipe the diner counter, and smirks. "Autumn confetti and questionable life choices-must be-fall."

"Autumn confetti — that's what she calls it.
The leaves start falling, and suddenly the whole town loses its mind. Pumpkin this, cinnamon that, scarves the size of blankets. Every latte order comes with an emotional breakdown and at least one questionable life decision.

I've seen it a hundred times — folks come in here pretending it's about the weather, but really, it's about the change. Something about fall makes people restless. They chop their hair, they text their ex, they decide to start candle-making businesses.

Me? I just pour the coffee and watch the madness. Because in this town, when the leaves start to fall, the stories start to rise."

"Marvin, you make fall sound like a crisis hotline, " Lucy says, learning across the counter with a smile. "It's not chaos; it's character development. Leaves fall, hearts open, and sometimes a person just needs to impulsively buy a dozen pumpkins and a life-size scarecrow named Reginald. That's not a questionable life choice-that's commitment." She stirs her coffee dramatically. "Besides, if we didn't make at least one bad decision every fall how would we know it's working?"

Lucy looks out the window, watching a gust of wind carry leaves down Maple Street like glitter tossed by the universe. "It's autumn confetti, Marvin. The universe is celebrating and you're just grumbling about the cleanup."

Suddenly Floyd remarks, "since autumn confetti appears to be allowed, does anyone know if pumpkins can legally wear sequins? I signed up on the sign up sheet for the Pumpkin Pageant."

Lucy, still sipping her coffee, nods. "See, Marvin? Exhibit A of autumn magic- Floyd is turning projects into performance art."

Marvin lets out the kind of sigh that could power a windmill."Y eah, great, confetti. You know what I call that? Yard work." He grabs a rag, wipes the counter, and shoots Lucy a look. "Every year it's the same thing — you people turn Fall into a festival of insanity. There's glitter on my pancakes, someone's dog's wearing a cable-knit sweater, and now apparently pumpkins need costumes." He gestures toward Floyd. "Sequins, Floyd? Really? They don't even have shoulders."

He pours another cup of coffee and mutters, "You all act like fall is a religion and caffeine is communion. Meanwhile, I'm over here trying to keep the leaf blowers out of the diner."

Then, softer, he adds just loud enough for Lucy to hear, "But... yeah. Fine. Maybe the confetti's nice. From a distance. Preferably someone else's yard."

Floyd straightens his scarf, completely unfazed by Marvin's sarcasm.

"Actually, Marvin, pumpkins *do* have shoulders if you believe in them," he says earnestly. "You just have to tilt them at the right angle. It's all about perspective—and glue guns." He flips through his clipboard with intense focus. "Besides, sequins catch the light better at dusk, and if I'm going to host the Pumpkin Pageant, I refuse to let my gourds look underdressed. It's a matter of civic pride."

He looks between them, dead serious. "I'm thinking of adding a talent round. Maybe interpretive rolling or a pie-eating exhibition, that would go well with the pie throwing contest. Marvin, you'll provide catering with the hot dog food tent and hot dog contest.. And yes, I've already submitted the paperwork to the town council—under 'seasonal enlightenment.'"Lucy hides a laugh behind her coffee. "Floyd, you're a one-man autumn parade."

Floyd beams. "Thank you. I prefer the Grand *Marshal of Fall.*"

Poppy the bakery store owner swept into the diner in a flurry of whirlwind charm, curls, and cinnamon. She's holding two mismatched mugs and what appears to be a pie that didn't survive the journey.

"Did someone say *questionable life choices?*" she chirps, sliding into the booth beside Lucy—with a grin. "Because I just spent my entire morning making fifteen pumpkin pies for the Book Club kickoff, and then I remembered the club doesn't meet until *next week.* So either I'm incredibly prepared or I've officially lost track of time. Again."

Marvin eyes the pie, skeptical. "What happened to that one?"
Poppy waves a hand. "Gravity. She's fine. A little rustic. We'll call it a free-form *autumn confetti pie.*"

She turns to Lucy, eyes bright. "Also, I signed- us up to do the Bakery and Book Club Booth at the Fall Festival. I may have promised live music and matching aprons."
Marvin groans. "Of course you did."
Poppy beams. "Marvin, don't be such a maple leaf in a puddle. It's fall! It's festive!

Chapter 2

FALL FESTIVAL FOLLIES

Just as Floyd recovered from saving the day, he had to pass out the newspapers. Oh look he even remembered to give you a coToday wasn't just any day-it was the beginning of the Fall Festival Follies. The town was already humming like a hive about to bust with stories.

The morning seemed perfect-sunny, crisp, and calm. Lucy was busy buzzing around-pumpkins garnished the town everywhere with cinnamon aroma from Poppy's Bakery. Lucy balanced a tray of Poppy's pumpkin scones while trying not to trip over a wandering dog that seemed quite friendly. The booths were being set up, pies, scones, muffins, cookies, and butterscotch popcorn balls.

Lucy, the busy multitasker, had convinced her assistant Michelangelo to help run the Book Club and News Booth while Poppy promised pastries.

Marvin swore he'd stay sane serving breakfast to half the country. Lucy's two daughters were helping Marvin as he promised them free Marvins Diner Best Coffee on the Planet tee shirts.

Lucy's mother Moira was hosting the Ladies of High Tea and Low Gossip Charity. Moira gestures towards the floral settings and linens. "I've instructed the staff that the cucumber sandwiches are to be cut diagonally-triangles are more forgiving for conversation. If anyone feels like mentioning rumors, please ensure they're at least interesting ones. Nothing ruins an afternoon tea faster than a mediocre scandal. Because really, if one is going to talk about people, it should be done gracefully over porcelain, not in a supermarket aisle in joggers."

Lucy strolling by hears her mother speaking to her booth buddy from the High Tea and Low Gossip Charity. Lucy swoops in remarks, "what have I missed."

Moira responds, "Lucy, please try not to slouch. This is High Tea and Low Gossip, not a truck stop."

Lucy responds, "Oh, I must've missed the sign at the door that said no personality allowed. Don't worry, I'll keep my elbows and my opinions off the table."

Moira responds, "You could at least pretend to appreciate the culture."

Lucy responds, "Oh, I do! Nothing says culture like silently judging people while nibbling on overpriced lettuce."

Moira responds, "This High Tea is a celebration of refinement. A place for meaningful conversation."

Lucy responds, "Right-like how Mrs. Benfordell pearls are real, but her personality isn't."

Moira responds, "Lucy!"

Lucy responds, "Relax mom. Low gossip, remember? I'm just following the theme-keeping it tastefull."

Floyd was running around discussing the parade line up, checking in the booth participants, and trying to find his dog that he thinks is playing hide and seek. Suddenly a "BOOM, POW, BAM" light explosion and smoke! Floyd started running to see what happened.

Mrs. Lu was shouting for extension cords, as she was trying to keep the dumplings warm. The current extension cord overheated and Dr. Mr. Lu accidentally dropped his hot tea kettle all over the cord and the ground. By the time Floyd approached Mrs. Lu, she was already frustrated with the limited space available for her hot tea, matcha, and ice cream-not to mention the hot food dishes. Floyd finally was able to get Mrs. Lu calmed down, found more cords and expanded the booth space. Just watching the mishap, the clothing booth lady walked over and put a bright red cape on Floyd. She told him he was the Fall Festival Hero! Mrs. Lu clapped and smiled. Even the dog was found and began barking.

THE BEAN HIVE GAZETTE

Previously in Bean Hive Cottage:

The leaves turned gold just Lucy finished painting the last letter on in Bean Hive Cottage sign. The town was buzzing over the upcoming Fall Festival – a weekend of t booths, pie contests, parades, and enough go sosin, to fuel Mrs. Lub teapot for a month. Lucy, ever the multitasker, had convinced her assistant Michealangedlo to help run a Book Club & News Booth "tonics" Floyd prepared his apothecary "tonics" and M-Marvin swore he'd stay sane serving breakfast to half the county.

THE SQUIRREL IS THE TOWN MASCOT ONCE AGAIN!

Poppy's Bakery Specials
20% OFF ALL BAKERY ITEMS THIS WEEK

Apothecary has new products for new products
Once again!

Other News,
Bean Hive Cottage is looking the next book club event, sign u up with Lucy soon.

Marvin's Diner
BUY 1 COFFEE GET 1 COFFEE FREE

Marvin's Diner

Apothecary has new products once again!

Other News
If looks like a strong turnout for the Fall Festival. Please join us.

The weather will be a perfect sunny, crisp East Coast day.

The weather will be a perfect sunny, crisp East Coast Day.

Across the square, The Bean Hive Parade float was being built with the enthusiasm of a Broadway show and the structural integrity of a Jenga Tower. Mayor Bernie Ooglemyer stood on a crate, megaphone in hand. "Folks, remember! Safety first! Also-does anyone have extra glitter?"

Poppy waved from her bakery booth-a swirl of curls and powdered sugar. "Lucy! Do you want a test scone or are you pretending to be organized first?" "I can multitask!" Lucy shouted back, though her coffee sloshed dramatically.

Marvin, behind the hot dog tent, snorted. "You call that multitasking? I call that an insurance claim waiting to happen." He wore his apron like armor, the backwards baseball cap shading eyes that had already seen too much frosting.

"Marvin, you're supposed to be smiling today," Lucy said, passing by. "Festival rule number one."

"I'm smiling on the inside," said Marvin.

Mrs. Lu appeared with a tray of steaming buns from her Asian-Fusion Cafe, her husband the doctor following with a cooler of first aid kits-because Bean Hive Festivals have a certain track record. "Lucy!" Mrs. Lu called. "Try this!" It's pumpkin spice mochi. Limited edition."

Michelangelo muttered, "she says that about everything."

Lucy bit into one, eyes widening. "If heaven were chewy, it would taste like this."

"Put this on the sign," Mrs. Lu said proudly, turning to greet another line of customers.

The Scarecrow Contest was already attracting a crowd. Floyd somehow had managed to give his entry a scarf that smelled suspiciously herbal, while Miss Betty's scarecrow wore tap shoes. Mayor Bernie adjusted his glasses. "Creativity counts people!" he announced. "Just maybe not movement."

Mine's interpretive," Miss Betty said. "He expresses the fragility of harvest."

"Mine," Floyd added, "Keeps mosquitoes away and improves your aura."

Marvin leaned toward Lucy. "Remind me why we let them near hay and open air again?"

"Because this town would riot if we didn't." Lucy said.

Meanwhile the pie table gleamed like a pastry battlefield waiting for the pie throwing contest to begin.Dozens of whipped cream masterpieces sat in neat rows, labeled "Pumpkin," "Apple Cinnamon," and "Highly Questionable Blueberry."

Poppy stood behind the table, hands on hips. "No one touches these until judging time! Especially you, Floyd. Last year you started throwing the pies before the judges could judge how far and messy the pie toss was. Floyd says, "it's not a pie toss until someone wears the filling." Poppy laughs and says, "Be careful this year, the blueberries bruise easily."

Meanwhile hot dogs and havoc were happening, as Marvin's tent looked like the condiment booth of war. Mustard streaked all over the banner sign, as a kid knocked over the mustard pump, which exploded across the table like a yellow geyser, splattering everything within a ten food radius. Even a guest in a corduroy jacket! The twelve gallons of chilli cheese became a condiment crime scene, not to mention the sour cream cups didn't stay chilled on top of the ice. The ketchup bottles rolled across the ground, the chili cheese got so messy a customer stepped into a puddle of chili cheese on the ground.

Then the heroic dive off the folding table after someone tripped on the extension cord that was powering the slow cooker full of sauerkraut.

Lucy's daughters, Annie and Olive were first responders, offering first aid from slips, spills, burns, and handing out free vouchers at the diner. It was like a slow motion disaster movie: Marvin lunging, the pot from tipping sauerkraut, cascading spills, and the unfortunate bun slip.

Miss Betty screamed, someone had slipped on a bun. Marvin was busy on the grill as 150 people were in line for hot dogs. Now these were not just any hot dogs, these were hot doggies wrapped in bacon! Poppy noticed Miss Betty yelling for help and waving what appeared to be white napkins with ketchup and mustard spatter. As Poppy was running over, so was Dr Lu to the rescue.

By now Lucy was watching, and snapping photos for the newsletter. Marvin glared at her,"what are you doing?" Before Lucy could respond, there went the dog, running through the tent with a hot dog in his mouth and the plastic table cloth connected. Suddenly the messy white splattered table cloth turned into the hot dog slip in slide.

Lucy was doubled over laughing, tears streaking from her cheeks. "You've officially invented the Bean Hive Sip, Slip and Slide! Should we charge admission?"

Marvin glared at her, chili dripping off his baseball cap. "You think this is funny?"

"Of course it's funny," she gasped. "You're one ladle away from opening a theme park called Condiment Kingdom."

Just as he started to answer, the tent pole gave up entirely, collapsing like a tired umbrella. The banner fluttered down in slow motion, landing right on Marvin's shoulders-you could see the words on the banner so perfectly. "HOT DOGS, FAMILY FUN"

Lucy was narrating like the journalist writer she is."Breaking news! Marvin's Diner Fall Festival becomes the Mustard Massacre-eyewitnesses report chili-related injuries, and a home made condiment slip and slide created from a bun slip incident.The catastrophe occurred just after the hot dog eating contest."

The crowd gasped.

Mayor Bernie adjusted his glasses, staring at the mess in absolute confusion. You see he was on the float at the parade, and then he was watching the dance recital which- Miss Betty's dancers danced magically. He had no idea that such a disaster was happening.

Meanwhile the pumpkin pageant went well and the parade was great fun. Miss Betty's float had her dancers dancing, Marvin's Diner float had giant cardboard pancakes and coffee cut out. Since Marvin was cooking, he was not able to be on the float, so a Marvin cardboard cutout stepped in. Probably a good thing, especially since the unfortunate events that happened. Floyd had the apothecary float, and it smelled of cinnamon and maple. Mrs. Lu had her employees on her Mochi Ice Cream and Asian Fusion Cafe float, tossing out candy. Squire Squirrel continues to be the beloved mascot, he was on his very own float with the mayor. The Mayor presented Squire with his own brand new nut-house that has an unlimited peanuts, sunflower seeds, and corn kernels dispenser.

The annual Bean Hive Fall Festival was everything and more! Cozy chaos, with a little pumpkin spice. Maple street was thriving with vendors, laughter and the unmistakable smell of the hot dog shenanigans. Poppy's bakery was an all time hit, Lucy hit record high with new book club members, and Miss Betty's dance studio continues to get more and more talented every year.

Sunset, twinkling lights strung across the gazebo and into the town glowed. The smell of cider, the smell of spices, the hay rides, the pumpkins, Squire the squirrel, the magical togetherness of a place we all dream of.

Chapter 3

PUMPKIN SPICE PANIC

The scent of sugar and cinnamon drifted through Poppy's Bakery, wrapping around the sleepy town like a sweet autumn promise. The glass cases glittered with muffins, scones, and croissants stacked like little golden crowns. Behind the counter, Poppy stood in a swirl of flour and frenzy, whisk in one hand, phone in the other. "We're out," she whispered dramatically.

"Out of pumpkin spice." The words hit the kitchen like a thunderclap.

Lucy blinked from her stool by the counter, mid–latte sip. "Out? As in out-out?" "As if there is no blend left in this building, this town, or possibly the state!" Poppy wailed. "Fall is canceled!

Thanksgiving is doomed! My entire reputation is at risk!" She turned in a floury pirouette, bumping into a tray of cooling muffins that scattered like witnesses to a crime. Moments later, Floyd burst through the door, lab goggles still perched on his head, holding a steaming flask of something

suspiciously orange. "Don't panic," he said, grinning. "I've created a substitute—Pumpkin Spice Elixir T 2.0." Poppy sniffed it and coughed. "Floyd, this smells like nutmeg and... fear."

"Art,"he corrected proudly. "It smells like art." Marvin strolled in behind him, shaking his head. "If this turns into another hot dog situation, I'll call the fire department before the explosion."

The bakery bell chimed again as Mayor Ooglemyer swaggered in, wearing a tie with a turkey printed on it. "Poppy! Good news! You've been chosen to bake the official Bean Hive Thanksgiving pie." He placed a clipboard and an oversized pumpkin on the counter. "Press will be here Thursday."

The entire room froze. Lucy set down her coffee. "Poppy, breathe." Poppy inhaled a cloud of powdered sugar. "I can't. I'm hyperventilating in nutmeg." For a long moment, nobody moved. Then Lucy clapped her hands. "Okay. Operation Pumpkin Spice begins now. We'll find it, borrow it, or invent it—whatever it takes." Poppy's eyes

widened, hope flickering beneath the flour dust.

"You'd really help me?"

Lucy smiled. "We're Bean Hive. We survive chili spills, squirrel mascots, and Floyd's alchemy. We can handle a little spice crisis." Poppy straightened, tying her apron like armor. "Then let the pumpkin spice hunt begin."

Outside, the autumn breeze rattled the windowpanes as if to cheer them on.

Bean Hive has survived blizzards, bake-offs, and one very public interpretive dance protest (thank you, Miss Betty), but nothing sent the locals into such a frenzy as the words 'out of pumpkin spice.' Within an hour, news had spread faster than frosting on a hot muffin. Mrs. Lu started a

neighborhood thread titled 'Emergency Spice Situation.' The mayor announced an official 'Flavor Shortage Alert.' And poor Floyd, ever the optimist, offered to organize a town meeting to 'brainstorm alternatives,' which everyone agreed was the worst idea he'd ever had.

Meanwhile, Poppy's Bakery became a headquarters for chaos. A steady stream of concerned citizens arrived, offering everything from imitation flavoring to suspicious brown powders

in unlabeled jars. 'That's cumin,' Lucy said flatly to one man holding a spice shaker. 'Pretty sure that's how wars start.' Still, Poppy accepted every offering with gratitude, placing each potential substitute on the counter like a soldier in the spice army. 'If I mix them all,' she muttered, 'maybe I'll accidentally

summon Martha Stewart.'

Marvin stopped in from the diner with a tray of half-eaten pancakes and his usual deadpan expression. 'I tried to tell people we serve maple syrup,' he said, 'but apparently that's a crime this season.' Lucy rolled her eyes. 'You're just mad they

called your pancakes "emotionally dense."' He shrugged. 'Not my fault the batter matches my personality.' Poppy giggled in spite of herself, tension melting into laughter. That was the

magic of Bean Hive—crisis never stood a chance against community sarcasm.

As the day stretched on, the group gathered at the big farmhouse table in the back of the bakery. Recipe books were stacked high, cinnamon sticks littered the surface, and Floyd's bubbling flask sat in the center like a ticking time bomb. 'Maybe,'

Lucy said thoughtfully, 'this isn't about spice at all.

Maybe it's about spirit.' Poppy blinked. 'Lucy, I love you, but if we serve pie that tastes like spirit, the health department will close us down.' Just then, the doorbell jingled again. Everyone turned as Miss

Betty swept in, her dance bag slung over one shoulder and her hair perfectly pinned. 'I heard there's a shortage,' she said dramatically. 'Well, lucky for you, I hoard essential oils.' She produced a tiny glass bottle labeled Pumpkin Harvest Dream. 'We can bake with that, right?'

Floyd reached for it eagerly, and Lucy groaned. 'Absolutely not.'

Poppy just smiled—because in Bean Hive, even a disaster could feel like home when everyone

showed up to help, no matter how ridiculous their solution.

By late evening, the crisis had officially reached 'town-wide emergency' status. The mayor had drafted a notice titled 'The Great Spice Shortage of Bean Hive' and insisted on pinning it to the community board. Poppy rolled her eyes as she wiped down the bakery counter.

'You'd think we were out of oxygen, not allspice.' Marvin, perched on a stool with his coffee, grunted. 'Same thing around here. You can't breathe without fall flavor.'

Lucy had turned the back room into a makeshift command center, complete with sticky notes, recipe cards, and a wildly inaccurate spice inventory chart drawn by Michelangelo. Floyd hovered nearby with a notebook labeled 'Pumpkin Spice Experiment No. 7,' muttering something about molecular ratios

and emotional flavor frequencies. Poppy wasn't sure if she should be impressed or concerned. Probably both.

Just when it seemed the day couldn't get any more absurd, Mrs. Lu arrived with a mysterious wooden crate from her cousin's import shop in Boston. Inside were ten small tins labeled 'Autumn Blend.'

The room fell silent.

'Could it be...?' Poppy whispered, clutching one like it was sacred treasure. She twisted the lid open and inhaled. The scent of nutmeg, cinnamon, and salvation filled the air.

Lucy cheered. Floyd cried. Marvin muttered, 'About time.'

POPPY'S
BAKERY
OPEN

POPPY'S
BAKERY

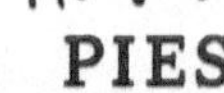

PASTRIES

 Butter Croissant
Almond Croissant
Chocolate Twist
Cinnamon Morning Roll
Blueberry Muffin

COOKIES

Brown Butter
Chocolate Chip
Oatmeal Cranberry
French Shortbread
Sugar Glazed Hearts

PIES

 Classic
Pumpkin Pie
Pecan Maple Pie
Strawberry Rhubarb
Lemon Meringue

BEVERAGES

Fresh Brewed
Coffee
Vanilla Chai Latte
Café au Lait
Hot Cocoa
Sparkling
Lemon Tea

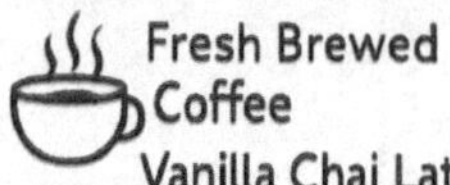

☆ SEASONAL SPECIAL
The Bean Hive Blend Latte
infused with caramel drizzle and cinnamon foam

POPPY'S
BAKERY

Chapter 4

BOOKS, BREWS & GOSSIP

Morning sunlight slanted through the cottage windows, painting golden stripes across the Bean Hive Book Club sign. Inside, the air smelled faintly of cinnamon coffee and fresh paper — Lucy's

favorite combination. She stood at the front counter, juggling two calendars, three emails, and one rapidly cooling latte. "Michelangelo," she called, "we have a tiny scheduling hiccup." From behind the espresso machine, her ever-patient assistant

looked up warily. "Define tiny," he said, already bracing himself. Lucy sighed. "Two retreats, same weekend. One virtual, one in person. Both at Bean Hive Cottage." Michelangelo blinked, then groaned. "Please tell me you're joking." Lucy shook her head. "Do I look like a woman who has time to joke?

The Boston Literary Society booked the upstairs reading room for Saturday, and the Cozy Quill Club booked the garden patio for Sunday. Plus we have the 47 Readers Anonymous Guild Guests staying 14 days at the Inn. For some reason 4 of those days we have The High Tea & Low Gossip Charity staying. Except — they both think they're staying overnight." Michelangelo rubbed his temples. "So... we're hosting twelve novelists, eight romantics, three mystery writers, and one woman who only drinks tea steeped by moonlight. Then toss in your mothers High Tea & Low Gossip Charity for the bonus." Lucy grinned. "Exactly! It'll be fine — if Poppy ever confirms dessert."

Just then a stranger walks into the door. Lucy grins. "Hello, how can I help you?" The man stands silent, looking around. "Greetings, I'm Theo Remington of Eastern Wesley University and I am inquiring about just what this Bean Hive Cottage buzz is?"

"Well, I am Lucille Huckelbarel, the owner of Bean Hive Cottage. Where we have monthly book club meetings, virtual book club events, social gatherings, book club retreats at our very own Bean Hive Cottage Inn, and a members club newsletter if you wish to sign up?"

"Yes, I need to sign up and I wish to book the Bean Hive Cottage Inn for a book club retreat, as well as join the monthly book club. My members have read your books and have been talking all about this interesting Bean Hive Buzz"

Lucy smiled, and helped Theo get signed up. "Have a great day, I will see you next month with your book club group."

Theo replied, "good day Lucille, and thank you."

Down the street, Poppy's Bakery was in full pre-retreat chaos. "You want how many tarts?" Poppy cried into the phone, her

blonde curls bobbing as she scribbled notes. "For which group? The ones who only eat gluten-free or the ones who think butter is a spiritual experience?" Lucy laughed. "Both, apparently."

Poppy groaned. "Oh, sweet croissant crumbs... I'll have to pull an all-nighter." Marvin, passing through with a tray of sandwiches for catering, chimed in dryly, "Just make sure you label everything this time. Last retreat I served the vegan group the bacon quiche." Poppy threw a dishtowel at him. "They loved it!"

By late afternoon, the cottage buzzed like its namesake hive. Virtual guests from as far as London joined via laptop while locals trickled in for the in-person event.

The walls glowed with fairy lights, and the smell of warm pie drifted from the bakery next door. Lucy set out name tags, bookmarks, and small gift bags tied with twine. "You've really turned this into something special," Michelangelo said softly, adjusting the mic for the livestream.

 Lucy smiled, a little shy. "It's not just about books —it's about belonging. People come here to feel seen. Even if it's just over a cup of coffee and a good story."

Halfway through the evening, Mayor Ooglemyer stopped by to deliver his "important town update," which quickly became the headline gossip of the night. "We're considering adding a stop sign at the corner of Maple and Almond," he announced.

The room erupted. "A stop sign?" gasped Mrs. Lu. "We've never had one there!" Marvin muttered, "We've also never had people who forget how to look both ways." Floyd chimed in from the back,

"To be fair, the ducks don't follow traffic rules." The mayor adjusted his glasses. "It's for safety! The geese have nearly caused two pileups, and last week a turkey blocked the intersection for ten minutes."

"Ten?" corrected Miss Betty dramatically. "There were eighteen turkeys in my yard alone! They strutted in like they owned the place." Laughter rippled through the cottage. Someone mentioned the wild animal sanctuary nearby, another bragged about blue jays stealing their peanuts, and soon the book club meeting had turned into an impromptu nature symposium. Lucy just leaned back in her chair, smiling. Bean Hive had its quirks— many of them feathered — but it was the kind of place where everyone cared, even about geese.

As the night wound down, the last of the guests sipped cocoa by the fire, and the virtual members waved goodnight from their screens.

Lucy and Michelangelo stacked chairs in comfortable silence. "Two retreats, one weekend," he said. "Think we can pull it off?" Lucy nodded, glancing around at the cozy chaos.

"Barely. But that's the charm of Bean Hive — it's never perfect, just perfectly ours." Outside, the streetlamps flickered on, and the faint sound of geese echoed from the pond — the town's unofficial lullaby.

The next morning, the scent of roasted coffee and maple scones drifted through the cottage as Lucy sat at her writing desk, surrounded by a clutter of ink pens, sticky notes, and half-finished headlines. The Bean Hive Gazette deadline was looming, and her mind was juggling between articles about the bake swap, the mayor's stop sign debate, and the growing concern about mice stealing café muffins. 'If journalism were pastries,' she murmured, 'this would be a twelve-layer mess.'

Michelangelo walked in with two mugs of coffee. 'You say that every week,' he said, handing her one. 'And somehow you still pull off a masterpiece.'

'Maybe,' Lucy replied, tapping her pen. 'But the Gazette's getting too big. Between book clubs, newsletters, and retreats, I can't even remember the last time I read a book for fun.' Michelangelo sat down across from her. 'You run this place like a symphony, Lucy. You're just forgetting to listen to your own melody once in a while.' She smiled softly, sipping her coffee.

'That's poetic. Did you steal that from one of the romance authors?' 'Maybe,' he said with a grin.

Outside, the morning bustle had begun. Marvin's diner sign flickered on across the street, Floyd's apothecary doorbell jingled, and the faint hum of Miss Betty's dance class carried through the crisp air.

Bean Hive was alive again — predictable and unpredictable all at once. Lucy opened the cottage window and smiled at the sight of Poppy hauling a tray of croissants to a delivery van. 'Don't forget my cinnamon scones for the afternoon club!' Lucy called.

'Don't forget my nap!' Poppy yelled back.

Later that day, Lucy hosted the 'Page Turners & Tea Leaves' club — a group of locals who read novels but mostly discussed who in town was secretly dating. 'It's not gossip,' insisted Mrs. Lu, sipping her tea, said, 'it's a literary analysis of real life.'

Marvin delivered sandwiches mid-meeting and stayed just long enough to hear Floyd passionately defending a plot twist involving a haunted pumpkin patch. 'This is my nightmare,' Marvin muttered, retreating with his empty tray.

By midafternoon, Michelangelo was juggling emails from potential sponsors for the next book retreat. 'We're getting interest from three publishers,' he said, scanning the screen. 'And one influencer who wants to film a segment called "Brews & Bookish Vibes."' Lucy nearly choked on her coffee. 'If she brings a ring light into my cottage, I'm moving to the mountains.'

'You say that,' Michelangelo replied, 'but you'd miss the Wi-Fi.'

As the evening settled in, Lucy sat by the fireplace with her laptop, updating the Gazette layout. The flicker of the flames reflected in her eyes as she typed the headline:

'Bean Hive: The Town That Runs on Books and Caffeine.' She paused to glance at the framed photo on the mantel — the very first book club meeting, years ago. Back then, it had been six women, a plate of cookies, and a dream. Now it was a small empire of warmth, stories, and the occasional chaos — exactly the way Lucy liked it.

The morning of a retreat dawned crisp and golden, with a faint mist curling over the cobblestones as the Bean Hive bus rolled into town. Painted a soft robin's-egg blue with white trim, the bus looked more like something out of a storybook than a shuttle.

Its side read 'Bean Hive Retreat Express — Books, Brews & Bliss.'

Lucy stood on the cottage steps, waving as guests disembarked one by one — writers clutching notebooks, couples holding coffee cups, and a few shy newcomers looking around with delight.

'Welcome to Bean Hive Cottage!' Lucy called. 'Where the tea is hot, the books are better, and the gossip's free.'

Annie and Olive flitted around their mother like cheerful honey-bees, their matching scarves fluttering as they carried boxes of welcome packets. Annie, ever the planner, checked names off the list while Olive handed out warm muffins Poppy had baked that morning. 'You get bonus points if you can guess the flavor,' Olive said playfully to a guest. 'Hint — it's the season's favorite.' 'Pumpkin spice?' the woman guessed. 'Of course,' Olive grinned. 'This town practically runs on it.'

From down the lane, Floyd appeared — wearing an apron printed with tiny potion bottles — and pushing a cart stacked with glass jars tied with ribbon. 'Special delivery!' he announced proudly. 'Apothecary treat bags! Each one includes a calming balm, a lavender tea blend, and a tiny jar of courage.' Lucy arched her brow. 'Courage?' Floyd grinned. 'You'd be surprised how often writers need it.' Michelangelo snorted as he passed with a stack of clipboards. 'I'll take two.'

Inside, the cottage hummed with life. The fire crackled in the hearth, soft music played from the corner speaker, and Poppy's desserts gleamed under glass domes. Annie set out candles shaped like open books while Olive helped Floyd line the entry table with the apothecary gifts. 'I labeled each one with inspirational quotes,' Floyd said proudly. 'Though I may have accidentally put Don't Panic on the relaxation cream and Breathe Deeply on the cinnamon scrub.'

Lucy laughed. 'Honestly, that fits this crowd perfectly.'

By midday, the book club retreat was in full swing. Guests chatted at round tables, the scent of pastries and chai filled the air, and the sound of pages turning mingled with laughter.

Michelangelo managed the livestream setup for virtual attendees, occasionally muttering about 'Wi-Fi behaves like a cranky pigeon.' Lucy floated between groups, greeting familiar faces, introducing newcomers, and sharing stories from past retreats.

'It's amazing,' one visitor said. 'It feels like we've all been friends forever.' 'That's Bean Hive magic,' Lucy replied softly.

Out by the window, Annie and Olive sipped cocoa and watched as the mayor's car rolled past the square — the newly installed stop sign shining in the sunlight. 'Guess he won that battle,' Annie said. 'Yeah,' Olive giggled. 'But the turkeys are still crossing wherever they please.' Floyd, overhearing, chimed in from behind them. 'They're residents now. I'm working on getting them their own mailbox.' The room erupted in laughter.

As evening fell, Lucy gathered everyone around the fireplace for the final reflection circle. 'Each time you come to Bean Hive,' she said, her voice gentle, 'you bring your stories — and somehow, together, they stitch this town a little tighter.' Annie and Olive leaned against her shoulders, Floyd passed around the last of his tea, and Michelangelo recorded it all with quiet memories. Outside, night began to fall, coating the cobblestones and bus with a soft moon light glow. It was the perfect ending to another perfectly imperfect day at Bean Hive Cottage.

Lucy getting ready for guests at the Bean Hive Cottage Inn. She will have guests that stay for a week, a weekend, overnight, or just for the day. Regardless, you can count on great conversation, laughs, and fun.

Bean Hive Cottage Inn, book club retreats are a favorite. No matter if they are overnight or a day. "With plot twists and laughter by the fireplace. Where we curl up, read up, and spill the tea-literally."

Chapter 5

MARVIN'S DINER

In the middle of the night, the WEE-OOO, WEE-OOO of the Bean Hive Fire Department sirens erupted loudly. Suddenly, Marvin's Diner was on fire. Marvin woke up in a panic, half-dressed and barefoot, running down Maple Street with his baseball cap on sideways and his spatula still in hand. Smoke was curling out the diner windows like ghostly ribbons, and the smell of burnt biscuits hung thick in the chilly air. When the Bean Hive Fire Department roared onto the scene, it was clear they were more enthusiastic than precision. Benny Loomis began yelling at Maynard who was driving, "stop, stop, you're gonna hit the pumpkins." It was a disaster, the truck went rolling into a pumpkin display. Scarecrows went flying across the lawn, into the town pond.

Benny Loomis powered off the fire truck, in a jump like a superhero, chaos followed like leaves in a gust of wind. The fire truck had rolled right into Mrs. Waverly's prized pumpkin display from the fall festival. The grand prize ribbon now hung crooked on the pumpkin sign. A mountain of orange gourds went tumbling across Maple Street like bowling balls.

Benny, trying to help, slipped on a runaway pumpkin, grabbed a scarecrow for balance, and ended up dragging the poor thing halfway across the gazebo lawn while shouting, " I got it under control!" Of course he did not.

Meanwhile Maynard, the other fireman was trying to restore order, though it looked more like slapstick than strategy. He had one boot stuck in a smashed pumpkin, the other tangled in a roll of caution tape, and he was shouting through his megaphone. "Put the fire out, put the fire out." When he finally freed himself, Maynard attempted to repark the fire truck, only to accidentally blast the siren again, sending half of the crowd ducking for cover. Mrs. Waverly came out yelling and running in hysterics, "what have you done to my pumpkin display. Why is your boot stuck in the pumpkin?" Maynard, attempted to explain that the truck accidentally ran into the display. While he jumped out in a hurry to put out the fire stepping into the pumpkin. Suddenly Maynard remembered, "fire I must put out the fire."

Meanwhile Tom had been putting out the fire, that's right. When the truck stopped, Benny Loomis and Maynard were in the front of the truck with all of the pumpkin chaos. While Tom, he was at the back. Tom simply just got out of the truck, grabbed the hose and got to work putting out the fire. He was on a mission and didn't get distracted with the pumpkin chaos.

Floyd was yelling something about using his "Kitchen Scent Neutralizer," while Mayor Ooglemyer stood on the curb giving speeches about bravery no one could hear over the sirens. Lucy arrived, flashlight in hand, shouting, "Marvin!

Did you light the fryer again for warmth?" Marvin just pointed helplessly toward the door as the smoke billowed like a haunted carnival.

Once the firefighters got inside, the real show began. Someone hit the whipped cream nozzle instead of the extinguisher, coating half the counter in foam.

Miss Betty ran over in her nightgown with her dance troupe in tow, announcing, "We can fan the flames with feather fans!" The teens in pajamas twirled around in slippers and worked nonstop using the giant feather fans until every ember fizzled out. When the smoke cleared, Marvin stood in the doorway—covered in soot, disbelief, drenched sweat—and muttered, "I should've opened a salad bar."

Meanwhile, the scent of smoke still clung faintly to the crisp East Coast air as Marvin stood outside his diner, flipping pancakes on a borrowed outdoor grill. The kitchen fire had been small but mighty enough to shut down half the diner and scorch his favorite cast-iron skillet. Now, wrapped in a flannel jacket and armed with a spatula, he muttered to himself about back orders, wiring delays, and the curse of faulty ovens.

Behind him, a crowd of hungry tourists wandered through Bean Hive, lured by the town's reputation as the must-see stop for fall tours.

Lucy had stopped by that morning, sipping her coffee and trying not to laugh as Marvin attempted to keep his breakfast line running with nothing but a griddle and optimism. She'd gently reminded him that her next book club retreat was coming up and—of course—his diner was in charge of catering. Marvin had rolled his eyes so hard it nearly qualified as exercise. Between the repair crew dragging their boots through the kitchen and Floyd from the apothecary trying to sell him some new "chemical miracle" cleaner called Kitchen Scent, Marvin was two coffee refills away from a full-blown meltdown.

Floyd, ever the salesman, swore his potion worked better than bleach and left kitchens smelling like "autumn renewal." Marvin wasn't convinced. "The only thing I need renewed is my patience," he grumbled, scrubbing soot off a counter that didn't even exist anymore. But Floyd just winked, left a free sample, and said, "You'll thank me when the critics start saying your pancakes smell like possibility."

Marvin considered tossing the bottle into the nearest trash bin—but supplies were low and possibilities, apparently, were free.

Just as he started to regain some rhythm with his outdoor setup, Miss Betty and her dancers paraded in, feathers and all. "We just need a little space to rehearse before the recital!" she chirped, her troupe of teens wobbling behind her in turkey costumes that looked one thread short of exploding. Marvin blinked. "This is a diner, not a barnyard." But Miss Betty was undeterred. The dance studio's stage crew was still building props, and she insisted his customers would love a little "pre-holiday entertainment." Marvin was not so sure. Miss Betty had explained with the fall tours happening, everything was booked full today. Marvin hesitated, "well okay, okay, go ahead just don't touch anything."

By lunchtime, a full audience of amused tourists filled the outdoor tables, cheering as the turkey dancers flapped past the grill.

Marvin stood amid the chaos—smoke curling, feathers flying, Floyd's cleaner fizzing on the counter—and wondered how Bean Hive managed to turn even disaster into a small-town theater. He sighed, flipped another pancake, and muttered, "Gobble gobble!"

Miss Betty wasn't one to do anything halfway. By midafternoon, she'd transformed Marvin's patch of pavement into a full rehearsal stage. Hooks, hoops, and a suspicious number of glittery feathers appeared out of nowhere. Her turkey dancers were now leaping, twirling, and attempting cartwheels that sent feathers floating like confetti. Marvin stood frozen by the grill, spatula in hand, as one dancer narrowly missed his coffee pot with a backflip.

"I'm running a diner, not Cirque du Gobble," he muttered, earning a round of applause from amused customers.

As if the performance wasn't enough, the smell of sizzling pancakes and bacon drew attention from an entirely different audience—Bean Hive's local flock of wild turkeys. They waddled into the park beside the diner, curious and bold, heads bobbing in judgment. One strutted right up to the stop sign, as if obeying traffic laws, while another took interest in a customer's plate of fries. "Great," Marvin grumbled, "now the turkeys have reservations."

Miss Betty saw an opportunity, of course. "They're perfect for realism!" she exclaimed, clapping her hands as her dancers squealed in delight. "Imagine how inspired the kids will be, performing with actual turkeys!" Marvin stared blankly at her, then at the birds, then back at her again. "Inspired? They're about to be chased."

Sure enough, chaos broke loose when one of the real turkeys mistook a sequined dancer for a rival. Feathers flew. Dancers screamed. Floyd ran out with his "Kitchen Scent" spray like a firefighter, insisting it would "calm their nerves." It did not. Instead, the cleaner hissed, the turkeys gobbled louder, and the tourists applauded like they'd stumbled onto a Thanksgiving parade.

The turkeys began to walk faster, while Floyd continued spraying the spray. A woman yelled, "that spray is making the turkeys angry, not calm."

Floyd just looked at her with a disappointed look on his face. Next thing, Floyd found himself in the circle of all the turkeys surrounding him. He dropped the spray and ran.

The mayor arrived just in time to witness a turkey standing proudly at the stop sign, blocking traffic with all the authority of a crossing guard. "Now that's civic pride!" Mayor Ooglemyer declared, clapping his hands.

Marvin, covered in flour and regret, looked skyward and whispered, "Take me now."

Lucy with notepad in hand, jotting every moment down for The Bean Hive Gazette. "You know," she said, smirking, "this might be your best publicity yet.

Breakfast, feathers, and free entertainment." Marvin shot her a look. "If you print one word of this, your next latte's coming burnt." She grinned anyway.

"Worth it."

As the sun dipped behind the orange-tipped trees, the chaos finally began to settle. Miss Betty gathered her troupe, the turkeys retreated to the park, and Marvin leaned against his grill, exhausted but oddly content. Bean Hive had once again managed to turn disaster into charm.

The laughter lingered in the air, warm and ridiculous, and Marvin couldn't help but smile. "Maybe next year," he said softly, "I'll just serve turkey sandwiches."

MARVIN'S
DINER

Chapter 6

CIDER DAYS AT BEAN HIVE APPLE ORCHARD

Cider Days arrived in Bean Hive like a sweet breeze of cinnamon and nostalgia. The air smelled of baked apples, wood smoke, and adventure. Buses lined the main road as tourists poured out, cameras in hand and scarves fluttering like autumn flags. Lucy stood near the Bean Hive Cottage sign with her Gazette notebook, ready to capture the heart of the town's most beloved event:

Cider Days at Bean Hive Apple Orchard.

Mr. Quigley's Apple Orchard has been a staple in the Quigley family for nine generations. Mr. Quigley, the cheerful owner of Bean Hive Apple Orchard, wore his usual red suspenders and a hat shaped like a giant apple. 'Pick a good one, folks!' he shouted as families scattered through the orchard rows. His wife's famous 'Apple Storytime' for kids was already gathering a crowd under the old oak tree, where Mrs. Quigley sat in a rocking chair telling tales of 'The Great Apple Tree of Sixty-Two'—the one that supposedly grew so big, that the tree produced enough apples for all of Bean Hive, and then some.

She told tales of the old farmhouse door that was built from the apple tree wood, and how the Quigley factory continues to produce apple fruit snacks, apple juice, and many other products today. Other guests signed up for the apple cooking class, always a favorite in the fall.

The Cider Mill was in full swing and the Apple Orchard was full of life with all of the tourists today. The kids gasped; the parents chuckled; and Mr. Quigley winked, as he greeted the visitors.

Meanwhile, the aroma of freshly fried apple fritters drifted through the orchard. Poppy was helping out, as Mr. Quigley is her uncle! That's right, Poppy's mom was a Quigley! So Poppy never misses cider days! She had set up a pop-up bakery booth covered in gingham cloth and tiny twinkling lights. 'Try my cinnamon-drizzled fritters!' she called out, waving her tongs like a carnival barker. Her table also boasted apple strudel dusted in powdered sugar and little cups of apple ice cream that melted faster than anyone could eat them. 'It's like autumn in a scoop,' Poppy said proudly, handing one to Lucy.

The Apple Orchard History Center, gives tours of the apple factory, cider mill, orchard, and a Quigley family history lesson. You see Mr. Quigley's family is a long lineage of apple orchard keepers-nine generations of Quigleys have tended the same rows of Honeycrisps, Empires, Red Delicious and Cortlands that continue to fill the Bean Hive Apple Orchard today.

Mr. Quigley's great-great-grandfather built the first cider mill by hand, using river stones from the nearby brook and wooden gears carved from fallen oak trees. Each generation added a touch of its own, a new press, a wider barn, the apple factory, history center, tours, then came the cider days events. Mr. Quigley continues to use his family's secret cider spice mix, and every autumn he feels the hum of family history in the creak of the old press handle. Folks say when he pulls the lever, you can almost hear the ghosts of the old Quigleys cheering on another good harvest.

Over the years, the orchard became more than a business-it became a gathering place. During the war years, the Quigleys hosted dances in the barn to lift the town's spirits, and when hard winters hit, they opened their cider house to neighbors who needed warmth and a hot cup. Mr. Quigley still keeps an old photograph on the wall that reminds him that the orchard's heart has always been about community, not just apples.

Crowds continue to roll in and visit, they sip cider, nibble apple delights from fritters, pies, muffins, donuts, scones, cookies, ice cream, and lattes. People love the laughter and joy each season brings to the orchard.

Mr. Quigley was asked why he does all this. Quigley replied "gratitude, and good cider, every apple tells a story, and ours just happens to have nine chapters of Quigley's and counting."

Meanwhile at Marvin's Diner, the day started with a breakfast special: apple pancakes, apple bacon glaze, and a brand-new drink Marvin called the 'Apple Latte.' He poured it into glass mugs with caramel foam on top and told customers, 'It's basically fall in a cup—with caffeine.' By noon, he was already testing a new creation: the Apple Pie Frappuccino.

It was the least he could do, after all, with the fall tours in full bloom, tour buses were coming daily, folks stopped off at Marvins as the shopping, entertainment, and tour groups needed refreshers and food. Marvin has been quite busy these days in which he seems to be warming up to the fall season and holidays just around the corner. Marvin has been so busy and being busy means making more money, so Marvin financially was able to hire two more employees to keep things going more efficiently.

Floyd stopped in to 'taste-test for quality control' and ended up bouncing off the walls after three of them. Marvin muttered, 'Next time, decaf.' The orchard was alive with laughter and music. The Bean Hive High marching band played classic fall tunes while the local quilting club sold apple-patterned potholders nearby on Maple and Almondale Streets.

Lucy interviewed guests for her Bean Hive Gazette feature, jotting notes about the town's charm and how 'no one does fall like Bean Hive.' She caught quotes from tourists who said the orchard looked like 'a postcard that came to life.' She smiled, thinking they weren't wrong. Many expressed love for the fall tours, where they were able to stroll along the wooden walkway bridge at Bean Hive, and see a theater play or dance show at Miss Betty's. Bean Hive does not disappoint.

One woman said, "Bean Hive is the most delightful magical place ever." Many guests were signing up for the Bean Hive Cottage Book Club, the most amazing, incredible book club ever.

The town was buzzing, the tour buses were hauling guests to Mr. Quigley's Apple Orchard and around Bean Hive Town. Guests were strolling around the parks, the shops, and feeding the ducks at the pond.

There were musicians and street vendors, and the visiting crowds found the events to be a magical delight.

By afternoon, the hayrides were in full swing. Mr. Quigley climbed up onto the tractor, waving to the kids who squealed in delight as the wagon rolled through rows of red and golden apple trees. 'Hang on tight, this is the bumpy patch!' he warned,

laughing as the wagon bounced. A little boy shouted, 'This is better than the fair!' while Lucy snapped photos for her Gazette article, the scent of cider wafting behind the wagon.

Meanwhile Annie and Olive, Lucy's two teen age daughters were busy helping at the kids apple bobbing, and apple cake walk events.

Cider Days are always a fun filled event, and Lucy was trying her best to capture every lovely moment.

As the sun began to set, the orchard glowed with strings of lights, the sound of fiddles, and the soft clink of cider mugs. Couples sat on hay bales, children ran through corn mazes, and the air buzzed with happiness.

Mr. Quigley raised his glass of warm cider and toasted the crowd: 'To good apples, good stories, and good people!' Everyone cheered, and the band played one last lively tune.

That night, as Lucy returned to Bean Hive Cottage to type her Gazette story, she could still hear the faint hum of laughter echoing through the town. Her headline read: 'Cider Days Bring Sweet Memories to Bean Hive.' She smiled, sipping a leftover apple latte, and thought to herself, some towns just smell like fall—and Bean Hive smells like home.

BEAN HIVE GAZETTE

CIDER DAYS BRING SWET MEMORIES TO BEAN HIVE APPLE ORCHARD

Mr, Quigley's annual Cider Days took place last weekend at Happy Hive Apple Orchard, where tourism has been booming. Many visitors have been traveling to Bean Hive to enjoy the fall colors and stop at the Cider Days event.

IN OTHER NEWS

Miss Betty has put together a wishlist for her next theater production. Please visit the town hall to see which items are needed.

CIDER DAYS

Chapter 7

FRIENDSGIVING

Lucy takes the medical emergency kit, "Gee thanks as always Dr. Lu, we can always count on you The morning light drifted through the kitchen curtains at Bean Hive Cottage, as a sweet gentle glow softened the room. Outside, the last of the golden leaves twirled across the yard, catching in the corners of the porch and the steps leading to Lucy's front door. Inside, the house smelled of cinnamon, butter, and something sweet that had been baking since dawn. Lucy wiped her hands on a tea towel and smiled to herself—this year, she'd promised to keep things simple. But, of course, "simple" in Bean Hive never lasted long.

Her mother stood by the counter, elbows deep in a bowl of mashed sweet potatoes, giving orders like a general preparing for battle. "Don't forget the marshmallows," she said. "The girls will never forgive you if there aren't marshmallows."

"I think they'll live," Lucy replied, her smile widening. "They're practically adults now."

Her mom raised an eyebrow. "Adults who still sneak cookie dough at midnight aren't adults, dear."

From the living room came the laughter of Lucy's two daughters, Annie and Olive, who were stringing popcorn garlands for the mantle.

Every so often, Olive would toss a piece into her mouth instead, and Annie would scold her before doing the same. Lucy's father Walton, outdoors on the patio smoking a cigar while drinking a scotch. He was enjoying a moment of not traveling, you see Lucy's dad is a business man and owns Bean Hive Bank, Bean Hive Real Estate, and Bean Hive Travel and Tourism.

It was the kind of morning that felt stitched together by memory—soft, unhurried, and wrapped in the smell of nutmeg and nostalgia. Since Lucy's husband (who was her high school sweetheart) passed away five years ago, she holds on to the memories and small moments even tighter. You see Lucy's husband was in the military and his plane went down on a mission. Ever since then, she embraced the Book Club Activities, Newsletter, and Bean Hive Gazette in full commitment. Perhaps it's due to being a mom, raising two daughters, or perhaps a good distraction, or fear of the unknown life without him. Regardless, Lucy is a strong, amazing, coffee espresso loving Book Club dreamer and doer.

Lucy paused at the window, watching the view and smiled at the town. She thought about how quiet the streets had been this week. Many families had packed up and left to see relatives across the coast, but not everyone had somewhere to go. That thought tugged at her heart—the kind of small ache that always made her want to make more pie than anyone needed.

She never liked quiet, brought back too much heart ache and hurt. She enjoyed having company around, the pure delight and laughter and music.

By mid-afternoon, the kitchen looked like a beautiful disaster. There were pies cooling on the sill, bread rolls in baskets, and a turkey that looked far too big for the oven but somehow fit after three tries and one prayer. Michelangelo had been over earlier to help set the table, leaving behind a trail of glitter from the "gratitude" place cards he insisted on designing.

Lucy's mother poured herself tea and said softly, "It's good, you know—what you're doing. Inviting everyone. Holidays can feel loud when you're missing someone."

"Lucy nodded, her throat tightening. She knew exactly and wiped a small tear drop from her eyes. Her mom gave her a hug, "now, now dear, each tear drop running drains the heart of lovefelt." That saying got to her every time and for some reason more this year. Lucy began to think about this old saying that her mother always would say. So she finally asked, "Mom, what do you mean when you say each tear drop running drains the heart of lovefelt?" Her mom replies, " Each teardrop running drains the heart of lovefelt-yet somehow, in that quiet ache, love proves itself most real. For it's only when we care so deeply that the heart dares to break open.

Every tear becomes a whisper of devotion, a memory of moments too precious to forget. Though sorrow softens us, it also reminds us that love never truly leaves-it simply changes shape, flowing from the eyes back into the sound, where it waits to bloom again."

Lucy responds, "do you think I will ever find love again, I mean am I even loveable with all the emotional baggage and overly committed life of my book club?"

Lucy's mother smiles softly, "Oh my dear, love doesn't ask for perfection-it asks for presence. You, with all your stories and scars, your over committed book clubs and tender heart, are not broken; you are beautifully human. The right person won't see your baggage as a burden-they will see it as the proof that you've lived, that you've cared deeply, that you've tried. Love doesn't arrive when everything is tidy and easy. Love shows up when we are real, authentic, messy, busy, and when we know we are still healing our hurts. Yes, you will find love again-beacause you have a kind heart". Lucy replies, "thank you mom, I needed that."

'Lucy thought of Poppy, who had kept her bakery lights on late every night this week, as though work could keep grief at bay. She thought of Marvin, who'd confessed he wasn't traveling this year—too many repairs, too many reasons to stay.

And Floyd—dear Floyd—who had cheerfully announced he'd "bring cider and charm," even though everyone knew what he really needed was company.

Just as Lucy finished setting out the last candle, her phone buzzed.

"Hey Lucy," Marvin's voice came through, warm but tired. "You sure there's room for one more stubborn diner owner?"

Lucy laughed softly. "You're family, Marvin. There's always room. Bring that stuffing of yours—or whatever survived your kitchen."

He chuckled. "I'll bring the good kind, promise. See you soon."

When she hung up, she caught her mother's knowing look. "You've got a soft spot for that one," her mom teased.

Lucy blushed and turned toward the oven. "It's called friendship, Mom."

"Mm-hmm," her mom hummed, mmm mmmmm unconvinced."

A misty rain began to flirt with the windowpanes, a knock sounded at the door. Lucy opened it to find Poppy standing there, wrapped in a burgundy coat, a pie tin trembling slightly in her hands.

"I wasn't sure I'd make it," Poppy said, her voice small but trying to stay bright. "I burned the first batch."

Lucy took the pie gently. "Doesn't matter. You made it—that's what counts."

Poppy's eyes glistened. "It's just strange, you know? First Thanksgiving without them, I miss my parents so much."

Lucy reached out and hugged her, the kind of hug that said everything words couldn't. "Then it's our job to make it a good one—for them and for you."

Poppy smiled faintly, and the two women stood there for a moment, the scent of cinnamon and cold November air between them.

Inside, the fire crackled. Olive and Annie darted to the door to greet "Poppy," and soon the kitchen filled again with laughter. Lucy's mom shooed everyone out of the way so she could baste the turkey, muttering something about "no amateurs near the bird."

Poppy settled into a chair by the fire near Walton. "You ever notice," she said, "how quiet grief is? It doesn't slam doors. It just sits with you."

Lucy nodded. "And sometimes," she said softly, "it lets someone else sit beside - until it feels a little lighter."

Walton smiles, with his scotch in hand-"Grief, isn't something you get over.

Grief is something you carry with you inside of your heart. Some days you hardly feel its weight, other days it's pressed hard against your heart, reminding you of times that mattered, people that mattered, maybe you mattered. But that's the kicker about grief, you can't see it, you can only feel it, and if your eyes are never open you actually miss out on grief's true lesson. You see grief does not vanish when people do, it just evolves entwined with our own present daily life stories that we begin to realize grief is part of the journey in life. -Just like happiness, and pumpkin pie. Hey Lucy, do you have any more scotch?"

Poppy suddenly asks, "So what does healing even mean, will I ever get over this deep hurt."

Walton smiles again with scotch in hand, waving his gold pinkie ring, "yes, healing just means you have gratitude, and those memories and life represent value. Remember love will always find a new place to live."

Lucy smiles, "love will always find a new place to live, I like that-I may need to use that tagline in a newsletter."

Everyone in the room began to laugh. Olive brought in some hot cider, "Cheers."

The clock ticked gently on the mantle. The cottage, filled with candlelight and warmth, felt like the safest place on earth.

By late afternoon, the sun slipped behind the pines, painting the horizon in soft rose and amber.

A hush settled over Bean Hive Cottage just before the flurry of footsteps began. There was a knock at the door. It was Floyd, balancing a wooden crate in each arm, filled with bottles. His scarf trailed behind him like a banner as he climbed the steps.

"Delivery!" he called, nearly tripping on the porch rug outside the porch. "Liquid gold straight from Quigley's orchard." Mr. Quigley regrets that he and the family are not able to attend this year; regardless I have a letter and gifts of joy for you.

Lucy smiled, and hurried to open the door before he spilled something explosive. "Please tell me that's cider, not one of your experiments."

"Both," Floyd said proudly, setting down the crates. "This one's spiced with cinnamon, this one's mulled with cloves, and this one"—he tapped the smallest bottle—"is what I call 'a leap of faith.'"

Her mother peeked from the kitchen. "Should I get the fire extinguisher?"

"Only if it starts glowing," Floyd replied, unbothered.

Laughter bubbled through the room. Poppy poured him a mug and raised it in mock salute. "To Friendsgiving," she said softly. "To make sweet new memories."

Lucy smiled, "cheers to the Quigley family, we will miss them this year. Cheers to health, wellness, and happy times."

The clink of their mugs sounded like a small promise.When suddenly Annie yells, "Wait just a salute! Come on we have cider mugs, what does mom always say? A hug and a mug are her favorite things! Come on everyone, get in here for the grand hug with our mugs." Lucy smiles with delight, giving her daughters Annie and Olive an extra hug with a fresh poured hot cider mug! Everyone raises their mugs, "cheers to hugs and mugs."

Laughter and smiles filled the room. Expressions of joy and hope for the season filled Poppy' s heart with a few tears. Lucy gave Poppy a hug.

The next knock at the door came with the familiar booming voice of Mayor Bernie Ooglemyer. "Permission to enter the residence of Lucille Huckelbarel!"

"You don't need permission, Mayor," Lucy said, smiling as she ushered him and his wife inside. "It's a community dinner, not a council meeting."

Mrs. Ooglemyer swatted her husband lightly on the arm. "I told you to leave the clipboard at home."

"I never leave civic duty behind," he said solemnly, then broke into a grin. "But I did bring my famous cranberry compote. I stirred it myself—once."

Lucy led them to the table where the food was gathering like a parade lineup. "We're honored," she said. "Even if you give a speech before we eat."

"Don't tempt him," Floyd murmured.

Everyone smiled. Olive ran up to Mrs. Ooglemyer, "will you be available on Friday afternoon for piano lessons". Mrs. Ooglemyer smiled, "yes Olive, stop by around 3pm and we will practice for your lesson." Olive smiled, and Mrs. Ooglemyer gave a big hug, then Olive ran to the piano to play some music.

Moments later, the door opened again, letting in a swirl of cold air and Miss Betty herself— resplendent in a sequined shawl and a red wagon filled with a tray of empanadas, tamales, nachos, dips, and a charcuterie board decked out in glitter and turkey feathers. "I come bearing gratitude and gluten!" she announced. "Everyone, please be aware—I'll be collecting thankful thoughts before dessert. And possibly choreographing them."

She handed everyone a theater card, with a skit, and another card for everyone to write a thankful thought.

"Not tonight, Betty," Marvin groaned, appearing behind her with a foil-covered dish and a weary smile. "Unless you can dance the potato polka."

"Challenge accepted," she quipped, walking in and setting her tray and goodies beside the turkey.

Standing behind Miss Betty in the doorway, it was Marvin smiling. Everyone was at the door looking at the cards Miss Betty handed out. While Marvin stood on Lucy's front porch shifting a casserole dish from one hand to the other as if hesitating, the foil crinkled like a nervous tic. The November air smelled like woodsmoke and cinnamon. Annie asked, "how about I help you with that dish, it looks super heavy and hot." The entire cottage stood still, just watching Miss Betty navigate all her goodies she brought, and Marvin's soft awkward moment. Marvin muttered, "it's just stuffing, not a Nobel Prize." Annie laughs, "Welcome to Friendsgiving, come hungry, leave hugged and mugged." Marvin laughed nervously. "Hugged okay but mugged I'm not sure about."

Lucy grinned, watching Annie take Marvin's dish. "Stuffing?"

"From scratch," he said proudly. "Didn't even burn it this time. My kitchen's still standing." Lucy smiled at the dish, brushed his sleeve with a grateful squeeze, and said, "Then tonight it's legendary stuffing." As Marvin walked in.

Moira sniffed the air. "Then we all have something to be thankful for."

Poppy was stirring gravy, Miss Betty arranging the cookies on the platter, and Marvin smiled.

Soon, the cottage was full—voices blending like the notes of a familiar song. Mrs. Lu and Dr. Lu arrived carrying a bamboo steamer of dumplings that filled the room with warm ginger aroma. Their daughter, Juniper, skipped in behind them with a paper turkey hat she'd made.

"Happy Friendsgiving!" she sang, holding it out to Lucy.

Lucy smiles to admire it. "It's perfect. Maybe I'll wear it during dessert."

"Good idea," Juniper said gravely. "It will make the pie taste better."

The room erupted with laughter again—gentle, genuine laughter that felt like sunlight after a storm.

Annie and Olive loved Juniper, they shared sweet greetings and began to run over to eat appetizers.

Dr. Lu never misses out on an opportunity to bring his medical emergency pack, he hands Lucy the medical care back. "Here is the medical emergency kit, just in case there are any cuts, burns, for all our unfortunate injuries."

Dinner took shape slowly, beautifully. Dishes covered every inch of the table—turkey, dumplings, roasted vegetables, sweet potato casserole, Marvin's stuffing, and Floyd's assortment of mysterious beverages. Candles flickered, casting little halos of light on each face around the table.

Lucy looked at the chairs—each one borrowed from various rooms in the cottage, mismatched, and perfectly right. Every person there had a story stitched to the night. Poppy's quiet courage, dealing with the loss of both parents last year. Marvin's steady presence, and always trying to make the best of things in his grumbling ways. Miss Betty's endless flair, for style, extravagance, and drama. The mayor's earnest heart, wanting to belong and always trying to help Bean Hive be the best town.. The Lu's kindness that crossed any distance, always available for medical needs, mochi, dumplings, laughs, and friendship.

For a moment, Lucy just stood in the doorway, watching everyone laugh and talk, feeling something that had no name but felt exactly like peace. Remembering what her dad always said, love always finds a new place to live. She also was starting to get a tear on her cheek, thinking of what her mother would always say, "love doesn't ask for perfection-it asks for presence."

Annie yells, "Mom, get in here, what are you doing standing in the doorway, get in here and give me a hug and a mug."

When the food was finally served, Miss Betty tapped her fork to her glass. "Before we eat ourselves into joyful oblivion," she declared, "we must say what we're thankful for. It's tradition."

Marvin groaned good-naturedly. "Here it comes."

"Go on, Marvin," Lucy teased. "Start us off."

He looked around, sheepish but smiling. "All right. I'm thankful for working ovens, loyal friends, and a town that somehow puts up with me."

"Add good coffee to that list," Floyd said, raising his mug.

Marvin pointed his fork. "You just want me to reopen early."

Laughter rippled around the table.

Poppy spoke next, her voice quiet but sure. "I'm thankful for second chances," she said. "For the kind of people who make the holidays less lonely. My parents used to say there's always room at the table—and tonight proved them right."

Lucy reached across and squeezed her hand. "Always," she whispered.

One by one, everyone shared something. The mayor gave a small, heartfelt speech about community and hope. Mrs. Lu spoke of kindness, Dr. Lu spoke of being thankful for no injuries and safety prevention, Miss Betty thanked "the divine energy that keeps us all just dramatic enough." Floyd toasted "to family—the kind you make, not just the one you're born with."

And when it came to Lucy's turn, she hesitated, looking around the table. "I'm thankful," she said softly, "for moments like this—when everyone's together, safe, and seen. This house was just a cottage once. You all made it a home."

Outside, the wind carried the scent of pine and the faraway hum of the harbor. Inside, the Friendsgiving feast glowed warm under golden lamplight. Someone turned on soft jazz from the record player, and the clink of dishes gave way to the rhythm of contentment.

Lucy caught her mother watching her from across the table, approval written all over her face. "You did great, my Lucy," she mouthed.

Lucy smiled. "We all did," she whispered back.

Just when the laughter was at its fullest and plates were nearly clean, a sharp knock rattled the front door. Lucy rose, brushing her hands on her apron. When she opened it, the November chill rushed in—along with George Seivert, the goat farmer from the outskirts of town. He was a kind quiet man, who was just crazy enough about goats. That's right, the goats were so important, he actually had some of his most prized goats live in his house.

He stood there with rain in his beard, a wool cap tilted sideways, his best pair of bib overalls and a basket cradled in his arms. "Brought Goat cheese," he said simply. "And, uh... maybe a goat."

Lucy blinked. "A goat?"

"Not inside," he reassured quickly. "She's out back eating the grass, and saw the squirrels. I thought she might like the company, besides you have the back porch so she can hang out in case it rains heavily. She seemed excited, she loves Bean Hive grass, it's different from the farm grass!"

Lucy looked perplexed, "farm grass is Bean Hive grass? Well okay, whatever you say."

"George," Lucy said, smiling as she ushered him in, "only in Bean Hive Cottage could you bring livestock to dinner and no one bat an eye."

From the dining room, Marvin called out, "Depends which course the goat's for!"

The whole table laughed as George stepped inside, setting his basket down. Inside were small wrapped bundles—handmade goat cheese labeled Best Before Yesterday in his scrawling handwriting.

He took off his coat, eyes wandering the room with quiet surprise. "Didn't think there'd be this many people," he said, voice rough but gentle.

"There's always room," Lucy said, leading him to a seat near the fire. "We were just sharing what we're thankful for."

George nodded, staring into the flames for a moment before speaking. "Guess I'm thankful for keeping the farm. The farm was rough this year—too much rain, too little help. Lost a few goats. Almost gave up." His voice faltered slightly, then steadied. "But then I remembered something my wife used to say. 'As long as something's growing, there's still hope.' So, I kept feeding what was left—plants, goats, and myself."

The room went quiet in that respectful Bean Hive way—the kind that held silence like a prayer, not a pause. Lucy's mother dabbed her eyes. Poppy sniffled. Floyd looked down, pretending to check his cider.

"That's beautiful, George," Lucy said softly. "Thank you for sharing it with us."

George shrugged modestly. "Just cheese and words. Both get better with age."

Later, as dessert made its rounds—apple pie, pumpkin bread, and Miss Betty's surprise empanada encore—the conversation drifted to favorite traditions and stories from years gone by. Mrs. Lu told a story about her first American Thanksgiving, when she mistook pumpkin pie for cheese pie and ate three slices before realizing it was dessert. Marvin admitted he once burned a turkey so badly he used it as a doorstop for a week.

Floyd proposed a toast—his final and most poetic of the evening. "To old friends, new families, and the beautiful mess that is Bean Hive Cottage. May our stories always overlap like too many chairs around one too-small table."

They all raised their glasses—some cider, some wine, some tea—and clinked them together.

Annie, Olive, Juniper, and Miss Betty all did a dance, theater skit that everyone rolled with laughter.

Mavin and Floyd joined in with charades and Bean Hive Trivia games.

The evening was full of heart and joy, everyone seemed cozy by the fire. The clean up could wait; the laughter could not. The girls sprawled on the rug, Juniper braided Olive's hair, and Annie read a page from Lucy's favorite old storybook aloud. Miss Betty hummed softly, a half-finished tune that matched the rhythm of the crackling wood.

Lucy leaned against the mantle, eyes drifting over each familiar face. It was imperfect, this life—patched together with grief, with laughter, with all the little mending stitches of friendship. Yet tonight, it felt whole.

Her mother came to stand beside her, holding two mugs of cocoa. "You know," she said, "your grandmother used to say Thanksgiving wasn't about the turkey—it was about who showed up to help carve it."

Lucy smiled, her gaze resting on the crowded room. "Then we did alright, didn't we?"

Her mom nodded. "Better than alright."

The fire burned low, casting soft gold against the windows. Outside, the rain stopped, quieting the town under a gentle fog hazed blanket.

George stood to leave first, going to the back yard to check on his goat. "Thank you for the invitation, it has been wonderful, if any of you need more goat cheese let me know."

The Lu's and Juniper hugged and waved good night. Miss Betty packed her tray, humming a show tune about gratitude. The mayor and his wife thanked Lucy for hosting "the most efficient dinner this side of city hall," and Floyd lingered last, handing Lucy one final bottle of cider.

"This one's called 'Hope,'" he said. "No experiments—just apples and patience."

Lucy smiled. "I think that's the best recipe there is."

He tipped his hat and stepped out into the night.

Poppy smiled, and said good night.

Olive and Annie said good night and ran upstairs to bed.

When the door finally closed and the cottage quieted, Lucy blew out the last candle. The faint scent of cinnamon and wood smoke filled the air one last time. The chairs all disheveled, the cozy blankets by the fireplace tossed back in the basket, the empty cider mugs on the end tables. She sat down for a moment, letting the quiet wrap around her. Thinking in her mind, "You can't have a mug without a hug" or "Small town, big hearts, and an extra drink of cider,"-ahh thankful for every moment she thought, the night really was about second chances of heartfelt gatherings with people that mean so much. May my cup overflow and my life never be empty.

From the corner, her mom spoke softly. "You know, it's funny. You spend years building a life, but sometimes it takes one night like this to realize—you're already living it."

Lucy looked at her, tears gathering but not falling. "I think you're right."

Her mother smiled gently. "I usually am."

They shared a laugh that melted into the hush of the fire.

Lucy's eyes drifted toward the window. Moonlight glowed under the porch light, and for a moment, she could almost hear the heartbeat of the town—steady, strong, and full of love.

"Happy Friendsgiving," she whispered to no one and everyone all at once.

Lucy's parents said good night,- and that they would see Lucy, Annie and Olive for Sunday afternoon luncheon.

Chapter 8

BOOK CLUBS AND BROKEN HEARTS

The rain had turned to a drizzled mess by the time Lucy's coffee pot finally sputtered to life. It was a chilly dreary day outside. She has already been awake since five, working on the news and book club events. The Bean Hive Cottage Inn had back-to-back retreats this week, her inbox was a minefield of unanswered messages, and the Bean Hive Gazette layout was due by noon. Even with an assistant, and sometimes her daughters would help with tasks, there was never enough time.

The cottage smelled of caramel latte, boiled eggs, bagels, and warmed apple butter. Lucy always tried to have a full breakfast in the mornings, no matter how busy the day. Lucy yelled from the hall, "Annie, Olive, breakfast is ready." From upstairs Lucy could hear the sound of her daughters arguing over hair straighteners, lipgloss, scrunchies, and jewelry.

"Mom! Olive took my sweater again!" Annie shouted.

"I didn't! It's mine!" Olive yelled back.

Lucy took a sip of her caramel latte, "mmm mmmm good." "she muttered to herself. "The brew that starts my day, from calm to my patience officially expired." Looking at all the tasks for the day felt overwhelming, but she knew she had work to do.

The girls came downstairs, grabbed breakfast, hugs and mugs, kisses and well wishes, and off to school they went.

By the time Lucy made it to the Inn's kitchen, her phone was buzzing with texts from Floyd about cider syrup deliveries, an email from Marvin about catering mishaps, and a voicemail from her mother that began with, "I'm concerned about your scheduling choices and the High Tea & Low Gossip Charity."

Lucy groaned. That phrase never meant anything good.

Her mother, of course, was not just any mother. She was the daughter of Margaret Harkins-Summers, a founding member of the High Tea Low Gossip charity—an organization that somehow raised money for local causes, while perfecting the art of polite judgment. Lucy's mother Moira, continued her mothers work, as the daughter of the founder. Lucy's father continues to be the biggest supporter and donor of the organization.

Lucy had inherited her mother's determination but none of her diplomacy. Where her mother attended soirées and luncheons, Lucy attended coffee-fueled book clubs with names like Mystery Mondays and Fiction Fridays. Her mother loves status, and charity events, not to mention recognition for being a member! Lucy would much rather curl up in a corner reading a good book.

At precisely 9:15, a black sedan pulled into the driveway. Lucy didn't need to look to know who it was. The car door opened, and out stepped her mother in a cream wool coat, pearls, and an expression that could curdle milk.

"Darling!" she called, sweeping into the doorway. "I was in the neighborhood."

Lucy blinked. "The neighborhood is thirty minutes away."

Moira waved dismissively. "Semantics."

Within seconds, she'd hung her coat, rearranged the flowers on the counter, and taken control of the kitchen like a visiting queen inspecting her kingdom.

"Mother," Lucy said, "I'm a little busy today."

"So I see," Moira replied, eyeing the stack of Gazette drafts, three open planners, and a tray of unglazed muffins. "You appear to be running a newspaper, a hotel, a book empire, and a bakery simultaneously. How's that working for you?"

Lucy smiled tightly. "About as well as your to do list."

There was a pause—then, to Lucy's surprise, her mother laughed. "Touché. Still, you're stretching yourself thin, dear. You can't pour from an empty coffee pot."

"Mother, it's called entrepreneurship."

"It's called chaos with branding."

Michaelangelo burst into the room, looking frantic and shirt half on. "Lucy, did you bring croissants?"

Lucy and Moira, just glaring at him. "What happened to you?" Moira asked with a harsh look. Michaelangelo began to straighten up and button his shirt. "I"m not going to ever host the Swinging Singles over Sixty Book Club again. When we ran out of croissants, they attacked me."

Lucy's eyes grew wide open with surprise, "they attacked you for running out of croissants? We have more coming, Poppy's on her way."

Michaelangelo sat down on the stool by the desk and started crying. "It was frightening, I have never felt so scared in all my life. One woman yelled at me, demanding the strawberry dream croissants, and another women grabbed my arm...demanding she has the raspberry, blueberry brie croissants. I just can't. There were 60 single women over sixty that were yelling at me, I can't go back in there. I refuse to go back in."

Moira listening suddenly says, "you should have known better, those vultures, you know Poppy makes those addictive butter infused berry croissants that you can't just eat one."

Poppy just stormed in with the bent box of disheveled croissants, "hey, I"m stopping and dropping, I gotta get back to the bakery all butter and jelly is breaking loose" and out the door Poppy went.

Michaelangelo picked up the croissants, "I'm going in, I am not going to let these women intimidate me" and so he built up courage, rolled up his shirt sleeves, flexed his muscles, and took the croissants into the book club.

Lucy turned to face her mother fully. "Okay, what's this about you here? You only 'drop by' when there's an agenda."

Moira perched delicately on a stool. "The High Tea Low Gossip charity is hosting our winter shopping event this weekend and we spoke about this weeks ago. We're short one co-chair, and since you've become so involved with the community, why not help out..."

Lucy's eyes narrowed. "No. I don't' have time for all this volunteer work"

"Oh, come now, it's for the children."

"It's for bragging rights," Lucy countered. "I don't have time for a shopping event. I have four book clubs, two retreats, one Gazette deadline, and zero functioning brain cells."

Moira smiled serenely. "Then this will be refreshing. A little retail therapy and social networking never hurt anyone. Besides, I will buy you whatever you want."

"Mother, last time I attended, someone tried to sell me a bedazzled teapot."

"And did you buy it?"

"Yes."

"Then it worked."

Lucy exhaled. "Fine. I'll stop by. But only for an hour or two. Why must you ask me to go to these things? Why can't you ask Annie and Olive to attend."

"Wonderful," Moira said, already scrolling through her phone. "Bring something sensible. Not that cardigan with the coffee stain. Don't worry, Annie and Olive will have a turn later, they already have been recruited for the Holiday Jubilee next month!"

Lucy rolled her eyes, pouring herself another mug of brew. "You realize, don't you, that I have to host the Mystery Monday book club?"

Her mother tilted her head. "The one with the woman who insists every novel is secretly about her cat?"

"That's the one."

Moira smiled sweetly. "I'll buy you a lucky horseshoe."

Lucy couldn't help but laugh. "Thanks, Mother. I'll need it."

Outside, the rain was flooding again. Floyd's truck rumbled by, honking twice, and Lucy waved from the window. The town was buzzing—coffee brewing at Marvin's Diner, Poppy arranging pies in her bakery window, Miss Betty rehearsing her dancers in the theater across the square.

Bean Hive had a way of humming even in the cooler months. But Lucy felt the hum turning into a blurr—too many projects, too many deadlines, too much of everything.

Her mother took a sip of tea, watching her closely. "You know, dear," she said softly, "I sometimes worry you're too much like me."

Lucy looked up, startled. "That's supposed to scare me, isn't it?"

Moira smiled faintly. "Only if you stop before the good part."

The High Tea & Low Gossip Charity shopping event was everything Lucy expected and nothing she wanted. Regardless, she was committed now and would help as she always does.

The High Tea & Low Gossip Charity day arrived. The ballroom of the Bean Hive Community Center gleamed with chandeliers and scented candles, each table displaying crystal brooches, silk scarves, or handmade soaps that all smelled suspiciously identical. A string quartet played softly in the corner, and the women of the charity circled like butterflies—if butterflies wore pearls and whispered rumors disguised as compliments.

Moira swept into the room as if she owned the place. "Smile, dear," she whispered. "You're representing me."

"I thought I was representing Bean Hive Cottage," Lucy said.

"Same thing, darling."

Lucy sighed, plastered on a polite smile, and accepted a glass of sparkling cider.

At one table, Mrs. Dalloway-from-down-the-lane cornered her immediately. "Lucy! I simply must book the Inn for our tea society. We're reading a thrilling new biography on Eleanor Roosevelt. Tragic ending, of course."

Lucy nodded vaguely, glancing toward the exit. Her mother was already deep in conversation with three women comparing bracelet carats. They were looking with the hand held microscope, as if they were jewelry experts.

She checked her phone—three missed calls from Floyd, two from Marvin, and a text from Olive that read: Mom, Annie used all the hot water again.

She texted back: Tell her to use the timer I bought, we have to all use our timed amount of hot water until it's fixed.

Olive texted back again, that Annie locked herself in the bathroom crying about a boy.

Lucy texted back, "oh for heaven's sake, tell Annie I've got cookies and life advice both slightly overbaked but still good."

Olive texted back, 'She says she doesn't want cookies, just a new life. Should I slide the phone under the door?"

Lucy texted back, "tell Annie I will offer unsolicited wisdom from grandma when I get back!:

Olive texted back, "thanks mom she's out of the bathroom!"

Lucy escaped the High Tea event after exactly sixty-two minutes—Moira had her coat waiting.

"Leaving already?" her mother asked.

"I have work," Lucy said. "And I think one of your charity ladies tried to sell me a diamond-encrusted bookmark."

"That's Edna. She's creative," her mother said with a fond smile. "I'm proud of you, you know. Even when you're frazzled."

Lucy blinked. "That almost sounded sincere."

"It was. Don't ruin it."

Lucy replied, "Good bye mom."

By the time she reached Marvin's Diner, the crowd had cleared out. Marvin was wiping down the counter, his sleeves rolled up, the smell of chicken and coffee thick in the air.

"Hello, Lucy," he said. "You look like you've fought a small war, you look tired."

"High Tea & Low Gossip," she said, sliding onto a stool.

He grimaced. "Oof. You okay?"

"Define okay." Lucy asked.

"Alive, caffeinated, and still capable of sarcasm." replied Marvin.

"Then yes," she said with a smile.

Marvin poured her a coffee and leaned against the counter. "You know, Lucy, you don't have to save the whole town every month, maybe just once a week."

"I'm not saving it," she said. "Just keeping it caffeinated."

"Same thing," he said. "But maybe take a breath once in a while. Even coffee needs a filter. We can't be everything to everyone and still expect the same results. I say, let the chips fall where they may, and life life-after all time is not a renewable energy."

Lucy laughed softly. "That might be the most Marvin thing you've ever said. I appreciate you, and I know you are well intentioned. I just can't stop now, I have come along ways to get to where I need to be."

"I have a few of those, momentum keepers is what it's call." he said, grinning.

Lucy asked for some take out burgers and fries to go, for her and the girls. Marvin tossed in some added onion rings, and cookies. Lucy was in a hurry, get food, eat, say hello to her girls and make it to the book club that night. The girls were running the club, and while that was fine it was a chaotic book club.

Back at Bean Hive Cottage that evening, chaos awaited.

The Mystery Monday club was already arguing about who in their latest novel "really did it." Someone spilled tea on the sign-up sheet, and another guest mistook the Gazette drafts for bookmarks.

Meanwhile, the Romance Readers Circle arrived early and accidentally joined the mystery group's discussion, causing one woman to dramatically declare, "Love is the real mystery!"

Floyd burst in carrying three bottles of cider and a look of panic. "We have a problem."

"Which one?" Lucy asked.

He handed her a printout of the Bean Hive Gazette proof. At the top of the front page, bold as daylight, were words she didn't remember writing:

[INSERT LOCAL SCANDAL HERE].

Lucy froze. "Oh no."

"Oh yes," Floyd said. "I may have hit 'send' before editing."

"Floyd," she said carefully, "please tell me this wasn't the version that went to print."

He smiled nervously. "Define print."

You see, while Floyd ran the Apothecary, he also helped Lucy and Michaelangelo sometimes with printing during the busy season. Perhaps he even added a few of his own remedies and advertisements in for the apothecary.

Before Lucy could respond, her mother entered through the front door—of course she did—holding the freshly printed Gazette in her gloved hand.

"Lucy," she said in her most formal tone, "care to explain why your newspaper is suggesting an unspecified scandal in the mayor's office? What is this all about? How, when, where, I need to know what happened? The High Tea & Low Gossip Charity will demand answers."

Lucy's eyes widened. "Oh, for heaven's sake, really."

"I rather enjoyed it," Moira said, smirking. "Kept everyone guessing and laughing at the same time. You know the kind of belly laughs, where you get a tummy ache and crying."

The book-club guests giggled. Miss Betty, who had somehow wandered in for her readers' dance rehearsal script reading club, declared, "If there isn't a scandal, we'll just make one. The show must go on!"

Lucy buried her face in her hands. "I live in a sitcom, that seems to be on replay daily. I can see the next headliner, "Get Ready for Bean

Hive's Daily Mash-Up." Sometimes myself or my staff, we all make mistakes and it's okay, after all it brings the best interest in the gazette. People are talking, and regardless it is going to be for good, bad or in between, they are talking, that's genius advertising."

Moria looking perplexed, "Well Lucy, I suppose accuracy was optional? How very Bean Hive Gazette of you. A sitcom I'm not sure about, -now a reality show seems more accurate depiction".

Lucy shrugged her shoulders, "Mom thank you for your calm response and supportive feedback. I was busy and I did not have time to proofread, so I let Floyd print and distribute. Look if the universe wanted perfection, it would have autocorrect. Think of it this way mom, it's not a scandal just a mini scandalette with mysterious intrigue."

"Lucy, newspapers are intended to inform, not confuse. Honestly, even the society page at the High Tea and Low Gossip Charity luncheons are more accurate. Your father nearly choked on his coffee, when I told him to consider it a cleanse brought on by your creative spelling."

Lucy appearing flustered, "Wow, okay, thank you, I will add this to the list of I'll be judged for page 9 of subsection B. Sometimes we mess up and I was delegating, Floyd usually checks these things, and I was not available to proof nor was Michaelangelo. Messing up is not the end, I like to think that this is conversational reading, perhaps I'll get more book club retreat bookings."

Oh Lucy, now there you go again, first you had Floyd delegated that was part of the problem. Whatever, you always seem to manage to create chaos without even leaving the house. I continue to nurture you, to help you, and what happens, either you have typewriter revolt, artistic interpretation, or embracing journalism as a mad libs fact sheet right on the front page."

Lucy crossed her arms and started to walk away, "Hey, at least it wasn't a menu item. People get violent about misspelled food. I'm sure you are thinking my legacy is ruined, please go ahead and send me sympathy flowers. I'm pretending it was just a quirky journalist moment, and sometimes when an accidentally creative moment happens people love it. Look Miss Betty loves it."

Moira smiled, "Lucy, you have turned a simple article into a town wide riddle congratulations. I suppose at least your father found it amusing, he did laugh, but you know we need to strive for excellence. I'm not angry with you, just cosmically and profoundly disappointed. I"ve already told the High Tea and Low Gossip Ladies to ignore the paper today, it was the only dignified option I had. I suppose at least you're consistent with your chaos and confusion seems to follow you like a pet."

Just then guests were arriving, Lucy smiled and replied, " love you mom, thanks for always knowing what I need."

Moira snickered then left the room to find Michaelangelo to confirm luncheon plans for the High Tea and Low Gossip Charity.

By 8 p.m., the book clubs had collided into one noisy, caffeine-fueled crowd. Olive and Annie were having quite a time trying to keep things under control. The Mystery readers debated plot twists with the Romance group, the Non-Fiction crowd fact-checked everyone, and the Virtual Zoom Club's audio looped on repeat: "Can you hear me now?"

Lucy stood in the kitchen, watching it all unfold—Floyd trying to fix the sound, Miss Betty demonstrating dramatic reading techniques, her mother correcting someone's posture, and Marvin dropping by with an emergency pie.

It was pure, perfect chaos.

Moira joined her by the counter, sipping cider. "You always made things a bit messy."

Lucy smiled. "You always did like to point it out."

Moira shrugged. "It's part of my charm."

Just when Lucy thought the night couldn't get any busier, her phone buzzed again. Two texts—one from the Mayor about the next town meeting, the other from George the goat guy.

Olive: I lost the charity raffle tickets.

Annie: Don't freak out but I bought a goat.

Lucy blinked. She showed the screen to Floyd, who was mid-sip of cider. He nearly choked.

"Is that a metaphorical goat or...?"

"No," Lucy said, rubbing her temples. "We're probably about to be proud sponsors of a real, live goat."

Across the room, Marvin smirked. "Well, at least it'll eat your paperwork."

Miss Betty clapped her hands. "We can name her Charity! It'll be symbolic!"

Lucy groaned. "I'm living in a farm-themed fever dream."

Ten minutes later the front door burst open, and George and the goat stumbled in—George clutching a receipt and carrying a cardboard sign that read Congratulations, Winner of the Goat Sponsor!

"Greetings," said George.

"Oh, no," Lucy whispered.

A small, ash-dusted goat peeked its head around the doorway, nibbling on the hem of George's coat.

"Baa baa...baa" replied the goat.

"Mom," Annie said, panicking, "what is happening."

George sits down with the goat in the cottage, "hello everyone, Lucy you have won the sponsor event! I am here to introduce you to the goat that you get to sponsor. I also want to thank you and your mother for doing such a wonderful thing for me."

"Of course," Lucy said flatly. "It's the Bean Hive Cottage way. Even the livestock are friendly."

Her mother, impeccably composed despite the chaos, surveyed the scene. "Well, at least it's not another boyfriend."

"Mother!" Lucy sputtered.

Moira lifted her tea cup. "I'm simply saying, goats are easier to train."

The room erupted in laughter—laughter Lucy didn't even realize she needed.

"So what is this sponsor a goat thing" Lucy asked?

"Well you see my goat cheese has become so famous, it's even reached New York City.

Floyd yelled, "New York City, see I knew it, it was just a matter of time before your cheese was noticed."

George smiled.

There was an investor that came to the fall tours recently and happened to find my goat cheese farm. The man was so impressed that when he returned to New York City, his business partners tried the cheese and asked about investing in my small operation here. There's just one catch, Marigold my goat is to attend a ribbon cutting event with cheese samples, and an operations inspector from New York City is coming. These investors are impressed with my cheese, but I am not a photogenic guy, as you can see I'm pretty rough around the edges.

Mayor Ooglemyer suggested I contact you. Just as I was about to contact you, I saw your mother. We talked about the wonderful Friendsgiving event that was held at the cottage. I explained to her what was happening, and she also recommended you be the sponsor. You don't have to do much, just show up at my Goat Cheese Farm, smile, attend the ribbon cutting and meet with me and the New York City investors. If you are concerned about the time you are not working, don't worry I will pay you for it." George smiled. Plus you will get a great amount of publicity for the Cottage, book club and events just by showing up for Marigold and I.

Lucy's mom suddenly chimed in, "Lucy is thrilled beyond belief and if there is anything I can do to help let me know."

George smiled, "thank you."

Lucy gasped, "yes mom, I appreciate you always looking out for me."

Lucy smiled "George, I'm happy to help you. You have the best cheese and I am humbled you thought of me. I'm currently a little bit busy right now, but I will call you tomorrow and we can talk about it."

Everyone was smiling and clapping.

When the last book-club guest left and Marigold the goat was safely munching hay in the mudroom, Lucy found Poppy sitting quietly by the fireplace. She held a mug of cocoa, eyes distant. Somewhere along the chaos of the evening, Poppy showed up.

"You okay?" Lucy asked, sitting beside her.

Poppy shrugged. "You know that guy I was seeing from the next town? The one who said he liked pastries, ice cream, coffee, music, long walks, cooking, shopping, painting, bookstores and deep conversation?"

Lucy nodded. "The one who thought Dickens was a type of pastry?"

"That's him. He ended it yesterday. Said I'm too 'busy with muffins, apron attire, pulled back ponytail and emotions.'"

Lucy smiled sadly. "That's ridiculous. Those are your best qualities."

Poppy laughed through tears. "Thanks. I just didn't want to be alone tonight. I'm sorry I snuck in."

"You're not," Lucy said, slipping an arm around her. "You're at Bean Hive Cottage. We don't go alone here. Just relax, we are all here for you."

From across the room, Moira watched quietly, something soft flickering behind her sharp gaze.

Later, when the cottage had finally quieted, Lucy found her mother in the kitchen unpacking a small box from her car.

"What's that?" Lucy asked.

"A peace offering," Moira said. She lifted out a gleaming, vintage brass book cart. "I saw it at the charity sale. Thought it might suit your little Bean Hive Cottage Inn."

Lucy's eyes widened. "Mother, it's beautiful."

Moira brushed off invisible dust. "Consider it an apology for meddling, you know I don't mean it."

Lucy smiled. "You don't have to apologize. You're a professional meddler, and I love you."

Her mother chuckled. "Occupational hazard of motherhood. You spend half your life teaching children to be strong, kind and confident, and then they use all that strength and confidence to argue with you about curfews, crushes and whether love songs are therapy. You can't win, only a sip of life's delight as we age and pretend we are okay with getting old. Once you master the detachment of feeling no longer needed as the child grows up and has a family of her own, life becomes the retirement plan. My charity events and organizations help fuel me from being an invasive mother."

They stood in silence for a moment before Moira added, softer, "You're doing a wonderful job, Lucy. Even if it looks like chaos from the outside. You thrive in chaos, it is a gift use it wisely"

Lucy blinked, caught off guard. "That... means a lot, Mother. I know I'm sometimes difficult and busy, and I do appreciate you"

"Don't get sentimental. It ruins my image," Moira said, but her voice cracked just enough to betray her.

The next morning, it turned from rain to drizzle to snow. Snow drifted past the window as Lucy sat at her desk, typing her latest Bean Hive Gazette editorial.

Snow has arrived!

She paused, rereading the final lines aloud:

Snow has arrived!!

"We survive broken hearts, busy days, and mothers who love too loudly.

We balance book clubs and bedtime stories, deadlines and dreams.

Maybe that's what keeps Bean Hive buzzing—

A town full of imperfect people who still show up for each other.

She hit- save, leaned back, and smiled.

From the yard came the soft bleat of the newly christened goat Marigold —followed by Olive shouting, "Mom! It's eating the mailbox again!" Seems George and Marigold the goat were out walking and stopped by to say hello.

Lucy laughed, grabbed her coat, and called out, "Add it to the Gazette under local news!"

Her mother's voice echoed down the hall. "And for heaven's sake, tell Marvin to make more coffee!"

Lucy smiled, slipping on her boots. "Yes, Mother."

As she stepped outside into the crisp morning, the cottage lights glowed behind her like a beacon of cheerful exhaustion. The chaos, the laughter, the love—it was all exactly how it was meant to be.

Chapter 9

A TALE OF BOOKS AND COZY NOOKS

The first snow of December fell like sifted sugar over Bean Hive Cottage, resting softly on the windowsills and the tips of the pine branches outside Lucy's window. Inside, the cottage glowed with lamplight and the faint crackle of the fireplace. The scent of cocoa, cinnamon, and paperbacks filled the air—a sure sign that book club night had arrived.

Lucy stood in the center of her living room, hands on her hips, surveying the cozy chaos. Pillows were stacked in corners, teacups balanced on saucers, and every chair in the house had been borrowed or rearranged to form a circle around the fire. It wasn't perfect, but it was perfectly hers.

"Mom, where do you want the extra blanket basket?" Annie asked, dragging a woven basket nearly her size across the floor.

"By the window nook," Lucy said. "If anyone gets cold, they can wrap up while they read."

Olive followed behind, her arms full of books. "I picked the prettiest covers," she said proudly, dropping them onto the coffee table with a thud. "Michaelangelo said the colors matter."

"Only because presentation inspires participation," Michaelangelo replied from the kitchen, where he was arranging cookies on a tray. His red scarf hung loosely around his neck, his zebra glasses fogged from the oven heat, and his plaid roll-neck sweater already too warm. "No one wants to discuss literature without sugar."

Lucy laughed softly. "You've got a point."

By six o'clock, the first guests began to arrive. Poppy swept in wearing a knitted beret and carrying a platter of scones dusted with powdered sugar. "They're lemon lavender," she announced. "I figured if we can't travel to Paris, we can at least taste it."

Marvin followed a few minutes later, balancing a coffee carafe and muttering about how his diner's espresso machine "didn't know what rest meant." He winked at Lucy as he set it down. "For emergencies only," he said.

The cottage soon filled with laughter, the clinking of mugs, and the rustle of turning pages. The book of the night sat in the middle of the table—*The Wind Between Pages,* a gentle story about community and second chances.

Lucy opened the evening the way she always did, with a quiet smile and a simple question. "What did this book make you feel?" and "What happens when you read, do you feel swept away into the story?"

There was a hush, then Poppy spoke first. "It made me feel... seen," she said. "Like even small lives matter in big ways. I also feel as if I am in the story, I get real invested in reading. I enjoy stories where I feel I am part of the story"

Marvin nodded thoughtfully. "Made me want to fix up that old corner booth at the diner. Give people a spot to think without being rushed."

"Now that," Michaelangelo said, "is personal growth."

The room chuckled, but Lucy just smiled. She loved this part—the pause between sentences, the way everyone leaned in as though words themselves had warmth. Words on paper were simply words on paper. When we read the words, and we allow ourselves to feel the words, we become captivated by the story. Words on paper stitched with sentences become the story. Stories become the adventure, and adventure becomes the meaning of what embraces our thoughts and minds. That is why the book club events are so amazing. The belonging connection to stories shared and friendships made. Everyone has a story, everyone has an adventure, and everyone who puts words on paper is telling a story. These stories are what Lucy loves so much.

Annie and Olive sat on the rug, listening quietly, occasionally trading secret smiles. For all the noise and bustle in Bean Hive, this was their favorite kind of night—the soft kind, the one where stories replaced screens and conversation stitched people together. It is the stories within the conversation, that create the stitching of emotions and connections that bring to life meaning and purpose.

Michaelangelo passed around mugs of hot cocoa, careful not to spill on the well-loved books. "This," he said dramatically, "is my contribution to literature—caffeine and sugar."

"Don't forget humor," Lucy said. "That's your specialty."

As the night went on, the discussion drifted from favorite quotes to favorite memories. Mrs. Lu shared how she used to hide library books under her pillow as a girl. Miss Betty confessed she once returned a play script five years later but claimed "it was worth the fine."

The laughter that followed was the easy kind—the kind that belonged only to people who knew one another's hearts. Where there was laughter, and authenticity.

When the fire began to fade, Lucy stood to add another log. The crackles and glow rose again, soft and golden fire flames dancing along the walls, resting on the spines of books. "You know," she said, "when I started this little club, I thought it was about reading. But it's really about belonging."

Everyone went quiet for a moment, nodding. Even Marvin, who never stayed sentimental for long, looked into his cup as if agreeing silently.

Annie leaned her head on Olive's shoulder. "Can we do this every week?" she whispered.

Lucy overheard and smiled. "Every week, every season," she said softly. "As long as there are stories, there'll be nooks waiting for them."

Michaelangelo began gathering plates, humming as he worked. "If every chapter of life had a meeting like this," he said, "the world might be a little less lonely."

Lucy looked around at her friends—at the warmth, the cocoa, the flicker of firelight dancing over open books—and her heart filled with something too big for words. The moment of moments, the emotions felt big, and purposeful.

"Here's to the stories that find us," she said finally. "And to the cozy nooks that keep us. May we always shine in our stories, and glow in our thoughts."

The room murmured its agreement, "Cheers" mugs lifted once more. Outside, the snow fell quietly over Bean Hive Cottage, wrapping the world in the same hush that filled the room—a hush made not of silence, but of nestled peace.

Chapter 10

THE GREAT DECEMBER STORM

The flakes came quietly, like polite houseguests knocking on the windowpanes of Bean Hive Cottage. By sunrise, the polite tapping had turned into an all-out takeover. The roads disappeared beneath a thick quilt of snow, and the sound of plows echoed through Maple Street like distant thunder. Marvin's diner posted a handwritten sign on the door: *"Closed Until Further Thaw. Coffee Still Hot (If You Bring the Generator)."*

Lucy stood at the Inn window, mug in hand, watching the storm build. She loved snow—the way it made Bean Hive look like a postcard—but this wasn't the flirty kind of snow that twirled prettily in Hallmark movies. This was the heavy, serious kind that cancelled plans and made sensible people hoard batteries.

By midmorning, Olive and Annie were outside helping Floyd shovel the walkway. "We'll clear it before the book club guests arrive!" Olive shouted through her scarf. Lucy smiled. She was busy with preparations for the book club guests, plus the added pressure of snow covered plans. Excitement was building.

Floyd's hat was already dusted white, and every few minutes he'd stop to knock the snow off the brim. The flakes clung to his coat, melting into little dark patches as he leaned on his shovel. The wind nipped at his cheeks, turning them a bright shade of cherry as he grumbled about the mayor's promise to "get better plows this year." Still, there was something peaceful about the rhythm of it all—the scrape of the shovel, the hush of falling snow, and the faint smell of woodsmoke drifting from Marvin's Diner down the street.

Lucy called out from the porch, offering him a mug of steaming cocoa. "You keep knocking that snow off, Floyd, and you'll never get done!" she teased. He smiled, took the cocoa with his mittened hands, and leaned against the railing. The snow was falling heavier now, blanketing the town square in white. Somewhere in the distance, the bell above the apothecary door chimed, and for a moment, Bean Hive felt perfectly still—like a postcard coming to life.

Annie and Olive appeared to be in a snow shoveling competition, shoveling so fast they started laughing. Annie was scooping up the snow and tossing, while Olive was trying to push the shovel as if a human snowplow scooting the snow. Regardless, they were trying to hurry so fast, they were slipping and sliding along the snow covered ground.

The old shovels scraped against the bricks, echoing through the quiet town like a rhythm of determination. The snow was slowly clearing, and Olive, Annie and Floyd were doing a great job. Lucy smiled in approval.

Olive dragged the salt bucket closer, sprinkling a path that would keep the guests from slipping.
Annie, ever the perfectionist, made sure each edge of the walkway was

squared and neat, as if they were preparing a runway instead of a front porch. Even though the snow was coming down, it was still charming and a warmth even in the coldest of winter.

The Bean Hive Cottage Inn sign, creaked with strong gusts of wind, its golden letters peeking through a growing veil of frost.

Across the street, Marvin was trying to start his snowblower for the fifth time, muttering words that would never make it into the Gazette. He was frustrated, and appeared very determined to get the snowblower up and running.

The engine sputtered, coughed, and gave a pitiful whine before dying again. Marvin gave it a look that could melt ice faster than the salt truck. "You've got one more chance, buddy," he warned, as though the snowblower could hear him. Floyd, leaning on his shovel, yelled out, "Try sweet-talking it! Machines around here only listen when you flatter 'em!"

Marvin rolled his eyes, across the street. "You can keep your advice, Floyd. Stick to shoveling. Last time I listened to you, I ended up with a goat in my tool shed." The remark sent Lucy into a fit of laughter from her porch, nearly spilling her cocoa. Poppy, watching from her bakery window, pressed her fingers to the glass and shouted, "Marvin, if that thing blows up, I'm charging you for the cupcakes it ruins!"

Finally, after a dramatic pause and one more pull of the cord, the snowblower roared to life—spitting snow, smoke, and something that looked suspiciously like confetti. The sight stopped everyone mid-motion. Marvin blinked, trying to make sense of the pink and gold paper swirling into the air. "Who fills a gas tank with party left-overs?" he barked. Floyd doubled over laughing, claiming innocence while Lucy tried not to choke on her drink. Lucy yelled, "that must be confetti stored in the garage from last year's New Year party!" Marvin smiled.

By then, the sound had drawn a few curious neighbors out onto their porches, watching curiously. Mrs. Dudley appeared in her robe and slippers, holding a clipboard yelling. "I'm filing a noise complaint." Marvin yelled back "Mrs. Dudley, it's okay, the snowblower was not starting, it's okay." Mrs. Dudley and her husband own the Bean Hive Meditation and Wellness Spa. Leave it to Mrs. Dudley, if anyone is going to notice any noise or anything, she will! She's always at the town hall meetings complaining about everything.

Marvin tightened his scarf, half-muttering as the snowblower sputtered to life again, belching out a puff of gray smoke that drifted straight toward Mrs. Dudley's porch. "You'd think I was running a rock concert out here," he grumbled, wiping frost from his eyebrows. The engine finally steadied into a steady hum, and he gave the handle a triumphant smack as if to show the machine who was boss.

Mrs. Dudley's robe flapped in the wind, the hem already dusted with snow. "Some of us are trying to meditate, Marvin Daniels!" she shouted over the growl of the snowblower. Her slippers squeaked in the slush as she waved the clipboard like it was official town business. "Do you have any idea how disruptive this is to the aura alignment sessions?"

Marvin blinked, barely hiding a smirk. "Mrs. Dudley," he called back, "the only thing misaligned right now is this driveway. Once it's clear, your aura can glide right into town without slipping." He turned his back to keep plowing, the snow flinging in neat arcs toward the curb. Every few feet, he could still hear her muttering something about 'vibrational balance' and 'municipal decibel limits.'

Across the street, Lucy peeked from her window, coffee mug in hand, watching the exchange unfold like it was another morning episode of *Bean Hive Live*. It was just another winter day in town—Marvin wrestling machinery, Mrs. Dudley threatened paperwork over noise and her alignment with the universe. The snow falling quietly over the chaos and calamity, continued as if nature was determined to make everyone see nature's beauty and peace.

Just as Marvin managed to steer the snowblower toward the end of the block, Mr. Olsen from the post office came trudging down the sidewalk, mailbag slung over his shoulder. He hit a slick patch of ice and nearly went airborne, arms flailing like a startled bird before catching himself on a parking sign. "Good grief!" he barked, steadying his hat. "You'd think the town could throw down some salt before sunrise!"

Marvin throttled down the snowblower just long enough to shout, "You all right there, Olsen?"
Mr. Olsen puffed, brushing snow off his sleeves. "I'm fine, but I swear this sidewalk's got it out for me every winter." He adjusted his bag and stomped on with a dramatic huff, muttering something about "hazard pay for postal workers in Bean Hive Post."

A moment later, Miss Betty appeared at the corner, wrapped in her signature fur-lined coat and holding a giant yellow feather like it was a magic wand. She waved it high in the air and called out cheerfully, "Morning, Marvin good to see you this find snow day! When you get a chance, I need my driveway cleared before the rehearsal!" Her red lipstick somehow remained perfect despite the snowflakes clinging to her curls. Her freshly press on eye lashes filled with snow, appeared as if added snow glitter.

Marvin gave her a lopsided grin and a mock salute. "Yeah, yeah, Miss Betty, I'll get there after the mayor's place and before the next blizzard hits."
"Don't you sass me, Marvin Daniels," she laughed. "I've got dancers in snow boots and a turkey costume crisis—don't make me add snowed-in sidewalks to my list!"

Marvin just shook his head with a grin, turning the snowblower back toward the street. The whole town, it seemed, was awake now—complaining, waving, slipping, and smiling—while the storm kept on falling, thick and relentless, like Bean Hive's own brand of winter chaos.

The snow kept falling, thicker now, but the laughter and noise carried down Maple Street. Even as the wind picked up, there was warmth in the chaos—a small-town kind of warmth, built from good neighbors, broken machines, and the kind of humor that made even a blizzard feel like a community affair. Floyd called out, "Don't worry, Marvin! By spring, you'll have that snowblower mastered!" Marvin just shook his head and replied, "By spring, I'm selling it to Floyd's Apothecary as modern art."

Floyd yelled, "it could be a great addition to my new fuzz remover spray. I could use the snowblower as the prop!"

"Oh, great, it just never ends," Marvin smiled and shook his head.

Miss Betty suddenly trudged by in her fur-trimmed boots, holding a thermos of cocoa and offering moral support instead of help. She was always extra, everywhere she would go. Just because a little snow drifted in, does not mean Miss Betty slows down or hibernates. Afterall the show must go on!

The mayor's truck rolled slowly down the lane, plowing what he could before the next band of snow arrived. The town's plow was out sanding, salting, and scraping. Even Squire Squirrel did his part, he managed to gather as many leaves to clean up before the wind gusted in.

Lucy peeked out from the front window, waving a hand and holding up a tray of steaming mugs—freshly brewed Bean Hive blend. Any-one? Anyone?

Floyd set his shovel down, grinning as the smell of coffee drifted through the cold air.

"Coffee break," Annie declared, brushing snow from her coat, "before we turn into snowmen ourselves."
The group gathered by the porch steps, hands wrapped around warm mugs as snowflakes melted on their lashes. The air was so cold that every laugh turned into a puff of white mist. Juniper came running over, "hello everyone, wanna make snow angels?" Next thing, Olive, Annie and Juniper were off to run in the snow and make snow angels. Then they decided to make some a Bean Hive Cottage snow angel family.

Just beyond the fence, the road to the inn was nearly buried, and they knew they'd have to clear it before any guests could get through at the back entrance. Floyd, Michaelangelo, and Lucy decided they needed Marvin to come with the snowplow. Many times Floyd and Michaelangelo will start shoveling and are able to manage the snow, but this year's is coming down so heavy they will need a plow.

Next thing Lucy sees, Olive, Annie and Juniper, pulling the red sled from the shed, using it to haul another load of salt and sand toward the driveway.
Even the town squirrel, Squire, scampered across the snowbank, cu-rious about the commotion.
By noon, the storm clouds deepened to a bluish gray, and the first rumbles of thunder-snow echoed over the hills. Marvin was able to get the snowplow through the driveway and back entrance across the road perfectly.

The Bean Hive crew kept working, side by side, determined that no amount of winter weather would stop book club from happening. One thing Lucy appreciated more than anything, was the strong commitment of the town, everyone truly wanted to make a difference and help each other.

Guests trickled in just as the wind began to howl. The *Bean Hive Book Club Winter Retreat* was fully booked—nine guests, all ready for five days of cozy reading, cocoa, and connection. The fireplace glowed, the smell of cinnamon filled the air, and Lucy was halfway through greeting the last couple when the lights flickered once, twice, then surrendered completely.

A beat of silence. Then someone muttered, "That's ominous."

"Don't panic," Lucy said brightly, though her stomach dropped. "We're going for rustic charm—unplugged edition! We have a back up plan, we always have a back up plan. Hey Michaelangelo, what is our back up plan again?"

Michaelangelo smiling."I will get the candles and we can think of this as a small controlled fire, fear not. Since we lost power, we might as well gain ambiance."

One guest replied, "I have a phobia and it is being in a room with people in the dark."

Michaelangelo winked, "I've gathered the candles, have no fear, the candle cavalry is here. Not need to worry about a phobia in the dark with people, just close your eyes and when you open them again, well we will have a timeless mood lighting event."

The guest just looked on with disbelief, "mood lighting event."

Michelangelo, smiled and walked away.

The guests laughed nervously, clutching their coats as the wind rattled the windowpanes. Outside, the snow fell harder, a curtain of white swallowing the driveway. Floyd appeared from the kitchen doorway holding three flashlights and a half-empty box of matches.

"Power's out clear to the square," he reported. "The mayor says the lines are down by the post office."

Lucy forced a smile. "Well, good thing we stocked up on candles, Michelangelo is passing them out as we speak. This'll just make every-thing... atmospheric."

Olive helped light the first few tapers, placing them along the man-tle where the flames shimmered like tiny amber stars. The fire popped, throwing a warm glow across the room as the storm roared beyond the walls. Annie passed out glow sticks, while the fireplace continued to glow.

Someone began humming softly—an old carol—and before long the room was filled with low, comforting chatter. Poppy's bakery bas-ket sat on the table, covered with a red-checked towel, still warm from the delivery.

Lucy passed around mugs of cocoa, grateful that the gas stove still worked. "At least caffeine and sugar don't need electricity," she joked, earning a ripple of relieved laughter.

Thunder grumbled far off, and the chandelier above them swayed slightly, its crystals tinkling like tiny bells. Floyd checked the window latch again. "If this keeps up, the road'll be gone by morning."

"Then we'll just make it the best snow-in book club retreat ever," said Michaelangelo cheerfully, curling up by the fire with a blanket and a copy of "I Smell *Fall*". "Nothing says book club like a winter storm power outage togetherness."

Lucy chuckled, her nerves easing as she watched everyone settle in—boots lined up near the hearth, mittens drying on the rack, the scent of cinnamon and cocoa blending with pine.

In the distance, a snowplow rumbled past, its amber light blinking faintly through the storm. It faded quickly, swallowed by the blizzard's white haze.

Floyd returned from the generator shed, shaking snow from his shoulders. "No luck," he sighed. "That old thing's frozen solid."

"That's all right," Lucy said, determined to stay upbeat. "We'll make our own light. Floyd, grab those lanterns from the storage closet, will you?"

As he left, Olive peeked through the curtain. "You can't even see the end of the walkway anymore. The cars are buried. We worked so hard to clear the paths today, and now it's all covered."

"Well," Lucy said, pouring herself a mug of cocoa, "Bean Hive Cottage Inn, has always been a retreat from the world. I guess tonight the world just decided to take that literally."

There was laughter again—genuine this time—and someone began passing around a deck of cards. The storm's howls became background music to their laughter, the soft thud of boots drying by the fire, the shuffle of pages turning.

Outside, snow piled high against the porch railings, covering the sign that read *Welcome to Bean Hive Cottage Inn*. Inside, the glow of candles danced across smiling faces, and Lucy realized something quietly magical: even in the dark, the Bean Hive Cottage, spirit never dimmed.

The next few hours were a blur of lighting candles, finding blankets, and pretending she knew what the breaker box was supposed to look like. One guest declared that "civilization officially ended when the Wi-Fi did." Lucy smiled through clenched teeth.

The guests appeared to feel comfortable, and the night cozy. The snow continued to fall, while the book club retreat continued on as a magical winter storm retreat.

Morning broke with a faint glow that seeped through the frost-coated windows, soft and silver, like the world outside had been erased and redrawn in snow. The storm had not let up overnight—if anything, it had doubled down. Drifts leaned against the doors, icicles hung thick as pencils from the porch roof, and the faint whistle of wind sounded like a ghostly lullaby through the chimney.

Lucy stirred on the sofa, her back stiff and her hair full of static. She blinked toward the hearth where the embers still glowed faintly orange. "Did anyone else make it through the night?" she croaked.

A few groggy murmurs rose from the quilts scattered around the parlor. Olive yawned and sat up, rubbing her arms. "We're alive. Though I think my toes froze somewhere around chapter five last night."

Annie, wrapped like a burrito in a plaid blanket, peeked out from under her cocoon. "Is it still snowing, wake me up when Spring arrives or Grandma comes?"

"Like it's got a grudge," Lucy said, peering out the window. All she could see was white—thick, endless, and blinding. The world looked swallowed whole.

She was about to turn away when a faint crunch echoed out-side—boots in deep snow. Then came a distant voice, barely audible through the glass. "Hellooooo in there!"

Olive gasped. "Did someone just yell?"

Lucy squinted and hurried to the door. The handle was near-ly frozen shut, but she managed to tug it open an inch, letting in a blast of frigid air. Standing knee-deep in snow were two familiar figures—Poppy, wrapped in her bakery apron and puffer coat, and Marvin, in his diner jacket and snow goggles.

"Breakfast delivery!" Marvin shouted over the wind, hoisting a steaming box like a trophy. "Special blizzard edition! I have enough food for breakfast, and lunch for you and your book club guests"

Poppy handed Lucy a giant box of pastries, and smiled with teeth chattering.

Lucy could have hugged them both right there on the porch if it hadn't been so cold. "You absolute angels! Now stay inside before you turn to icicles!"

They stomped through the door, snow tumbling off their boots. The smell hit the room immediately—fresh bread, warm bacon, cinnamon, and coffee so rich it could wake the dead.

Poppy grinned, cheeks flushed pink. "Bakery's got a generator, thank goodness. I made cinnamon scones, caramel rolls, and egg muffins. Marvin handled the hash browns."

"Handled is a generous word," Marvin grumbled, setting down a metal thermos. "Nearly lost half of 'em when the fryer sputtered. But we made it."

The guests gathered like bees to honey, eyes wide with gratitude. Lucy cleared the table while Floyd fetched plates and mugs, humming as if this were the grandest feast in all New England.

Steam curled in the air as everyone filled their plates. Someone poured cocoa; someone else lit a candle stub for light. For a moment, it felt less like being snowed in and more like being part of a grand winter adventure.

"Can't believe you two made it through that storm," Olive said, biting into a scone. "The roads are awful."

Marvin chuckled. "Roads? What roads? I drove through a snowbank, past a mailbox, and possibly a snowman. It's hard to tell the difference anymore."

Poppy laughed and elbowed him. "Don't listen to him, Lucy. He loves drama.

Lucy shook her head, smiling. "You both deserve medals. Or at least lifetime coffee tabs."

The fire crackled, filling the silence that followed. Outside, snow continued to drift lazily, but the tension of the night before had melted into something warm and content.

One of the guests, a writer from Boston, raised her mug. "To small towns and snowstorms. And to breakfasts that save souls."

Everyone clinked mugs and laughed. Even Floyd, normally so gruff in the mornings, cracked a smile.

Lucy looked around the room—at the friends, the guests, the breakfast spread that had turned a freezing morning into something magical—and thought, not for the first time, that Bean Hive Cottage had a way of turning chaos into charm.

Outside, the storm raged on, but inside, the laughter was louder. And as Poppy said with a wink, "If you're going to be snowed in, this is the place to do it."

Chapter 11

FLOYD'S APOTHECARY

Where strange remedies meet even stranger conversations.

Floyd Picklewitz (age 47) is Bean Hive's resident eccentric — the kind of man who smells faintly of eucalyptus, owns more scarves than sense, and believes the universe communicates through steam from his tea. He is an outgoing and friendly being, with just enough of this and over the top that. He appears to know everything and anything, if you have a need or want he can fix or find a remedy. He loves creating potions, and loves helping others. While most of the time he is well intentioned, the mishaps and follies seem to collide. Floyd is everywhere at Bean Hive, helping Lucy with her Bean Hive Cottage Inn, as well as the gazette printing and distribution. Floyd has staff at the apothecary, who seem energized and eager to help with what ever new idea Floyd comes up with.

Floyd has quite the resume, and keeps Bean Hive residents always curious as to what he will come up with next.

He's the owner of:

Floyd's Apothecary & Curiosity Shop

A tucked-away storefront between Poppy's Bakery and Marvin's Diner. The shop's hand-painted sign reads:

"Remedies, Rejuvenation, and the Occasionally Ridiculous."

Floyd grew up in Bean Hive but left for several years "to study herbal alchemy and emotional aromatherapy," returning mysteriously with a van full of jars, herbs, and theories no one fully understood. No one in town knows if he's formally certified in anything — but somehow, his potions work just enough to keep him in business. Floyd is one of Bean Hive's more interesting residents, let's learn a little more about him.

The shop feels like stepping into a potion bottle that never got fully rinsed. Shelves overflow with jars labeled in loopy handwriting: "Happiness Tea," "Courage Tincture," "Fog Be Gone Face Cream," and "Serenity Salts."

Dried herbs hang from the rafters, and a faint whiff of cinnamon and mystery fills the air.

There's a cozy back corner with mismatched chairs where Floyd hosts his "Thursday Therapeutic Teas" — informal group sessions that somehow end in laughter and mild confusion. The one interesting thing visitors encounter is his famous

Herbal Tea Testing Station

This is a curved wooden counter lined with mismatched teapots gently steaming like miniature cauldrons. Each pot is labeled with names such as Calm-Your-Mother-In-Law Chamomile, Stop-Overthinking Sage, and Picklewitz's Perpetual Optimism Blend. Guests may sample as many teas as they want—though locals warn newcomers not to mix more than three unless they wish to start speaking in poetic riddles like Floyd.

Floyd's inventory changes weekly depending on what he's "experimenting" with, but regulars can always find:

Dream Drops *- lavender and chamomile oil that's supposed to "make dreams cinematic."*

Bee Balm Elixir – *a nod to Bean Hive itself, said to calm anxiety and "boost creative buzzing."*

Mood Mist #7 – *a spray that smells like oranges, but Floyd swears it "removes negativity within a six-foot radius."*

Potion for Overthinkers – *peppermint and sage tea, comes with a note that says "drink before big decisions, like haircuts or dating."*

Foggy Brain Fix – *labeled "for writers, readers, and those who forgot why they walked into a room."*

"Floyd's Famous Foot Rub" – *not a product, just him offering unsolicited advice about proper footwear.*

Crystals, charms, and handmade soaps — *each with overly dramatic names like "Mercy Moon" or "Dawn of Calm."*

He also sells seasonal curiosities like:

Pumpkin Purity Powder (spoiler: it's cinnamon sugar mixed with ground pumpkin seeds)

Goat Milk Glow Cream ...inspired by George's farm-you see Floyd and George both love goats, and there are even times that Floyd will do magic tricks with George's goats. The glow cream is just that, it is a cream made from goat milk.

Bees Bean Hive Buzz Tonics (non-alcoholic, but suspiciously energizing, with local honeybees from Bean Hive)

To the right sits Floyd's Lotion Station, a cozy nook filled with creamy concoctions in glass jars of all shapes and sizes. Floyd claims every lotion is "emotionally calibrated," with scents like Courage-berry, Softening Sorrow Sandalwood, and I-Need-A-Nap-Immediately Eucalyptus-Mint. Regulars swear his "Warm Snickerdoodle Kneading Balm" works better than physical therapy, though no one knows if that's because of the cinnamon or the placebo effect. Funny thing about the Warm Snickerdoodle Kneading Balm, many customers buy it for their cats! Floyd likes to create multi purpose products, that way you are not just purchasing something for one ailment but multiple.

Floyd's Lotion Station isn't just a cozy nook with a table of creams—it's an entire glowing corner of the shop, lit with warm amber lamps that make every jar shimmer like tiny cauldrons of enchantment. Shelves are lined with hand-labeled bottles in Floyd's looping script, each promising its own peculiar magic: Peaceful Pomegranate, Grounding Geranium, Inexplicable Joy Juniper.

Visitors often describe stepping into the Lotion Station as a "mini vacation for the nervous system," thanks to Floyd's habit of piping soft wind-chime music from hidden speakers. He claims the sound "helps the molecules remember their purpose." No one knows what he means, but it's hard to argue with how calm the room feels. He also has that giant lotion bottle that says,

Floyd's Lotions and Potions, many customers come near and far just to have a photo of the giant bottle. I mean after all, how did he get a 15 foot life size lotion bottle into the apothecary?

Every lotion Floyd makes is "emotionally tuned," a process he insists involves reading the energy of the herbs while humming softly over the mixing bowls. His best-seller is the Warm Snickerdoodle Kneading Balm, said to soothe sore muscles and emotional flare-ups with equal efficiency.

Another favorite is Courage-berry Cream, which Floyd recommends before difficult phone calls, tense family dinners, or spontaneously signing up for Michelangelo's community yoga class. Each lotion has a consistency so velvety it feels like spreading kindness directly onto your skin—and customers swear that Floyd's blends genuinely lift the spirit, even if only because he insists they will.

No visit to the Lotion Station is complete without Floyd's "Mystery Sample of the Week", a small ceramic jar displayed proudly on a pedestal draped in velvet. The contents change every Friday and are always accompanied by cryptic directions such as "Apply before making a decision," or "Don't smell this until you're emotionally prepared." Some weeks, the sample is a calming lavender-lime cream that feels cool as morning dew; other weeks, it's a glitter-flecked balm that leaves everyone smelling faintly of stardust and possibility. People flock to the shop just to see what Floyd has concocted—because whether it works or not, it always sparks conversations, laughter, and a sense of shared curiosity that keeps Bean Hive feeling like the most magical town on the map.

One of the shop's most beloved—and most chaotic—features is the 3D Mirror Room, a small chamber filled with floor-to-ceiling mirrors and racks of eccentric clothing. Guests can try on scarves, hats, cloaks, capes, jackets, and an alarming number of fringed accessories. The mirrors multiply every angle, making it astonishingly easy for visitors to lose track of where they are. Marvin still tells the story of the time he wandered in looking for a scarf and emerged twenty minutes later convinced he had time-traveled.

Floyd insists the 3D Mirror Room "adjusts itself to match your inner vibe," though no one has ever confirmed whether he's joking. Some days the reflections appear unusually flattering, adding a subtle glow that makes everyone look as if they sleep eight hours and drink water regularly. Other days, the room seems to have a mischievous streak—elongating a hat here, multiplying a scarf there, or giving visitors an extra few reflections just to keep things interesting. Children from the Winter Book Club claim the room is "alive," and even adults admit the temperature subtly shifts depending on which rack of eccentric clothing you're exploring. The room appears to like a mirror maze, in which Floyd has a sign that states:

Enter at Your Own Risk-and Don't break the Mirrors

In the far corner sits the Disorientation Bench, a plush velvet seat meant for guests who need a quick reset after getting turned around too many times. Floyd added it after Poppy wandered in wearing a simple cardigan and came out wearing three scarves, two capes, and a pair of boots she swore were following her. The bench faces a single "normal mirror"—the one item in the room that behaves predictably—offering grounded reassurance before shoppers plunge back into the kaleidoscope of reflections. Visitors often linger there, laughing at the delightful absurdity of it all.

Because so many customers have gotten lost among the duplicated doorways, Floyd created what he calls the Picklewitz Path-Finding Protocol—a string of enchanted-looking lanterns hung along the ceiling that flicker softly to guide shoppers toward the exit. He claims the lanterns respond to intention: "Think 'out,' and they'll lead you out. Think 'fashion,' and you'll end up in the cape rack again." The townspeople tease him for this, but deep down, many believe there's truth to it. After all, Lucy once focused very hard on finding a cozy winter hat and ended up discovering a hat that, in her words, "chose" her. Whether magic or clever lighting tricks, the protocol keeps visitors both safe and thoroughly entertained—just the way Floyd likes it.

At the back of the shop, next to a shelf of dusty alchemy books, Floyd keeps his fruit, vegetable, and herb-infused jams and jellies. Flavors range from familiar (Blueberry Thyme) to polarizing (Spiced Carrot Sunrise) to outright suspicious (Emotionally Restorative Rutabaga). Yet locals swear that a spoonful of Floyd's Cranberry-Ginger Courage Jam is exactly what you need before a difficult conversation—or a karaoke night at Marvin's Diner.

Floyd's jams are rumored to be emotionally responsive, though he refuses to confirm or deny this. Residents swear the jars taste slightly different depending on your mood when you open them. Blueberry Thyme is known to be bold and bright when you're feeling brave, but soft and comforting when you're anxious. Spiced Carrot Sunrise has made people laugh unexpectedly, and Rutabaga Restore seems to develop a sweeter finish when someone is on the brink of tears. Whether this is science, magic, or simply the power of suggestion, no one knows—but shoppers insist Floyd's jars "meet you where you are."

Floyd claims his jams are preserved using a unique method he learned "from a monk who lived in the hills of Northern Somewhere." The technique involves simmering fruits and herbs under what he calls "intentional heat," which he describes as "a perfect balance between simmering and storytelling." He talks to the jars as they cool, whispering encouragement like, "Set gently, my little cranberry star," and the townspeople swear it's the reason Floyd's jams keep longer than anyone else's. In truth, Floyd says, "a jar preserved without joy is a jar doomed to mold."

The legend of Cranberry-Ginger Courage Jam has grown so strong that Bean Hive residents now keep a jar in their pantry the way others keep emergency flashlights. Over the years, locals have used it before job interviews, tough conversations, romantic confessions, and the dreaded parent–teacher meetings. Marvin once ate an entire tablespoon before proposing a new diner menu item; Poppy uses it before experimenting with bold pastry flavors; and even Mayor Ooglemyer famously took a dollop before giving his annual holiday speech. The jam has become a quiet symbol of bravery in the town—sweet, tart, and warm enough to remind you you're not alone.

Every spring, Floyd hosts Jelly Judgment Day, a tasting event where the community gathers to vote on which flavors will become part of the shop's limited-edition seasonal releases. The event features tasting spoons, tiny crackers, soft music, and a level of drama more suited to a reality TV show than a small-town herbal shop. People debate passionately over whether Cucumber-Lemon Clarity is "refreshing" or "oddly assertive," and last year's argument over Elderberry-Embers Essence nearly ended in a jam-throwing contest. In the end, Floyd tallies the votes, crowns a winner, and prints a special gold label that reads, "Blessed by the Bean Hive." The jars sell out every year.

On a small spinning rack, Floyd displays his line of lip balms that prevent sunburn, windburn, frostbite, and what he calls "first bite"—that nasty sting from the first cold winter gust that hits your mouth unprepared. They're made with beeswax, mint leaf, and what Floyd refers to only as "a whisper of hope."

Every season, Floyd unveils a new batch of experimental flavors, each one accompanied by a handwritten note explaining its "emotional resonance." In autumn, it might be Pumpkin-Clove Peace Offering or Maple-Mood-Lifter. In winter, jars of Frosted Pear Serenity appear on the shelves, shimmering with edible sparkles Floyd claims "enhance clarity of thought." Spring brings oddities like Dandelion Daydream and Minted Pea Motivation, while summer customers flock for the surprisingly refreshing Cool Cucumber Courage Jelly. Whether people buy them for the taste or the novelty, the shelves are rarely stocked for long.

Beside the jam display hangs the Picklewitz Pairings Chart, a poster-size guide Floyd created for customers unsure how to use his more peculiar creations. It suggests pairings such as Spiced Carrot Sunrise with warm biscuits, Emotionally Restorative Rutabaga with roasted potatoes, and Blueberry Thyme with "a moment of deep introspection or a view of the mountains at dusk." Despite the chart's unhinged logic, customers insist it works shockingly well, and the chart has become something of an attraction itself. Some even stop by just to take pictures of it for inspiration.

Once a week, usually around what Floyd mysteriously calls "the golden hour of taste," he hosts Test Spoon Hour, where courageous visitors can sample his newest concoctions. The line for this event often stretches past Marvin's Diner, as people come prepared with water, crackers, and—depending on the risk level—moral support. Even the bravest Bean Hive residents admit that some flavors are unforgettable in ways they can't fully explain. But every so often, Floyd hits on a combination so delightful it becomes a town staple overnight.

Legend has it that long ago, one of Floyd's earliest creations—Honey-Lemon Heart-Healer Jelly—helped mend an argument between two lifelong friends. Since then, Bean Hive residents have gifted Floyd's jams during apologies, confessions, celebrations, and even proposals. Now, every year during the Holiday Market, Floyd releases a limited-edition Unity Jar, a special blend that changes annually but always symbolizes harmony, togetherness, and the quirky spirit of Bean Hive Cottage. Families line up early to snag one, believing wholeheartedly that Floyd's jams aren't just food—they're a little bit of magic in a jar.

Next to a tray of herbal tinctures is a collection of Floyd's infamous soy-glass eyeglass readers. They're lightweight, biodegradable, and strangely durable. Floyd claims they "align your inner frequency so words appear crisp." Whether that's true or not, the frames come in delightful earth-tones, and no one can deny they make even the grumpiest reader look distinguished.

Floyd insists that choosing the right pair of soy-glass readers is not a matter of prescription, but energetic compatibility. When a customer tries on a pair, he has them stand very still while he circles them slowly, humming softly and occasionally squinting at the glasses as if reading invisible runes. Only when he feels the "vibrational match" does he give a satisfied nod and proclaim, "Yes, these will help you see both the world and yourself more clearly." Most customers buy the chosen pair out of pure curiosity—or because Floyd looks so proud of his process.

Each pair of readers comes with a tiny folded card titled "Proper Care for Energetically Sensitive Eyewear." The instructions include unexpected suggestions like setting the glasses on a windowsill during full moons, avoiding arguments while wearing them, and occasionally letting them "breathe" atop a houseplant. Despite the eccentricity, many customers swear their glasses really do feel lighter and clearer after following Floyd's recommendations. Poppy once confessed she placed hers next to her basil plant for a week and started writing recipes twice as fast.

Behind the reader's display is something Floyd calls the Clarity Wall, a large board where customers pin small notes describing what they were finally able to "see clearly" once they started wearing their soy-glass frames. Some notes are practical—"Finally found my missing measuring cups"—while others verge on mystical—"Realized I've been dating the wrong Harold for three months." The wall has become a beloved feature of the shop, filled with confessions, epiphanies, jokes, and heartfelt revelations from residents and tourists alike.

Despite their humble origins, Floyd's soy-glass readers have quietly become a fashion trend in Bean Hive. Earth-toned frames appear everywhere: at book club meetings, in the town garden, at Marvin's Diner brunches, and even during Michelangelo's sunrise yoga sessions. The mayor wore a pair during the annual Harvest Parade, declaring them "surprisingly stylish," and teenagers started buying them purely for aesthetic reasons. Whether or not they actually "align your inner frequency," one thing is certain—Floyd's readers have become an iconic part of Bean Hive's quirky charm.

Floyd is part philosopher, part town gossip, and part chaos in corduroy. He also loves art and when he has free time, he will paint and create wall pieces. Along the halls you see the art on display, and don't worry if you can't find what you want...
just ask Floyd!

I'm sure is is able to create exactly what you are looking for.

Floyd dresses like a cross between a Victorian botanist and a thrift-store poet. Always has a scarf, even in July.

His mannerisms and theatric gestures are like a production just watching him. He dramatically talks to his plants, and writes affirmations on sticky notes he sells as "Mood Cures."

Floyd exhibits many quirks, and insists his shop cat, Tonic, can detect bad energy; sometimes sells items labeled "Pending Scientific Approval (of the Universe of course)."

Catchphrases that are most common with Floyd:

"It's not weird, it's wellness-adjacent."

"Healing takes time—and a little bit of sparkle."

"Science is just magic that got its paperwork approved."

Floyd enjoys his friendship with Lucy, while constantly tries to get her to feature him in the Bean Hive Gazette. She finds him exhausting but oddly comforting. Floyd's relationship with Marvin can be a sitcom just watching the two of them communicate. Marvin calls him "the town witch doctor." Floyd calls Marvin "a skeptic with potential."

Floyd enjoys Poppy's friendship, as she tests all his teas but never trusts them—says they're "a bit too poetic to drink."

Floyd really brings the fun and magic to Bean Hive, with his wit, and funny apothecary products, you just never know what he will show up with next!

Chapter 12

HOLIDAYS AT BEAN HIVE COTTAGE

Snow blanketed Bean Hive Cottage in a soft hush that December morning, turning the little inn into a perfect postcard scene. Icicles glittered from the roofline, and smoke curled from the chimney like ribboned lace against the pale blue sky.

Inside, Lucy moved quietly through the parlor, lighting candles one by one. The scent of pine, evergreen and cinnamon filled the room, mingling with the faint snapping, popping, crispy crackle from the fireplace. The holidays had officially begun, and the cottage magic would soon be buzzing.

Poppy was already in the kitchen, nervously rolling out dough for cranberry scones. Her radio hummed carols, and she sang along with anxious excitement, completely off-key but perfectly happy.

Marvin stomped through the front door with a gust of cold air, his hat dusted in snow and a bundle of garlands under one arm. Looking pretty rough, and trying to rush. 'It's beginning to look like a lumberyard in here,' he said, grinning. "Where do you want the garlands, and I don't have time for small talk?"

'Don't complain, you never have time' Lucy laughed. 'You volunteered to hang them.'

'I said I might hang them,' he corrected, but he was already untangling a string of twinkle lights, stuck with a mix of tinsel and popcorn strings. The mix of holiday decor was all tangled and half of the lights didn't even work. Marvin appeared frustrated and continued on.

Floyd suddenly came in, balancing a crate of apothecary teas labeled Holiday Harmony, cinnamon passion, ice jubilee, and Snowfall Soother. 'Thought these might calm the crowd once the caffeine hits,' he said, winking. Mavin just grinned, "the only thing that will calm me down is January 2nd." Lucy began to laugh, "stop it Marvin, just stop it, you say that every year. What happens, you enjoy the holiday season more than you know. Think about the lights, the songs, the holiday connection. There is nothing like wishing your days aways, remember time is not a renewal energy."

Marvin gasps ...."days aways, is that even a word."

Floyd smiles, "it does not matter if you wanna skip the holidays and jump right into January 2nd, regardless I always have tea!"

Lucy laughed, "yes Floyd, you sure do"!

Marvin responded, "tea with crumpets, tea with soup, tea with gossip, tea, tea, tea, it always leads back to tea."

Floyd remarks, "what about tea, it just so happens that tea has many health and healing properties."

Then Lucy remarks, "tea is always best served with tea!"

Floyd laughed, "yeah your mother and her High Tea & Low Gossip group has the best tea...parties. You never know what hits the hottest, the tea or the tea."

Lucy laughed

Marvin signed, "tea this tea that it's always tea time at Bean Hive Cottage."

Miss Betty arrived in her usual grand fashion—red sequin velvet coat, purple feathered silver sequin hat, and a thick clipboard in hand. 'We need dancers! Carolers! Talent! Volunteers!' she declared before anyone could greet her. Her nails were all done up with red polish and purple tips.

Lucy commented on the outfit and told Miss Betty to go ahead and add a sign up sheet at the community board in case any visitors to the Inn wished to sign up.

Miss Betty expressed excited thanks and asked Floyd if he had any hot tea as it was cold outside. Just as she asked Marvin grinned and let out a shout, "TEA hell yes we have TEA, we have all the tea you want."

 Lucy laughed and walked away grinning.

Annie and Olive were perched on the staircase, threading popcorn garlands and giggling as they tossed pieces at each other. 'Don't eat the decorations!' Lucy called. 'We need every kernel!' Annie and Olive were trying to roll popcorn garlands and cranberries into the green garland. The task was exhausting as they were also putting up the gar-lands along the staircase and above all the doorways and then outdoors on the front and back porch. Annie and Olive decided to try to make it fun, and even wore half of the garland!

Michaelangelo entered last, arms full of clipboards and reservation lists. He rushed in in a panic!

'Five book-club retreats this week! All retreats, members are staying all week, plus the weekend events, and the weekly book club gather-ings, full capacity. Every bed, chair, and sofa was booked solid through New Year's.' We are going to be full, and we will need all hands work-ing.

Lucy's eyes widened. 'Five? At the same time?' 'You said Bean Hive Cottage could handle it,'

Michaelangelo replied. 'So now we're about to find out. Sure our usual meetings and events should work well...then again these retreats may get a bit over extended. I will do all I can to make everything work. I'm just saying, things may get a little over extended at times that's all. I got this don't worry."

Outside, the Bean Hive Cottage Holiday Market was already coming to life. To add to all the chaos and busy with the book club retreats, club events and gatherings, the holiday market was the biggest event of the season.

The hustle and bustle, the conversations, the decor, the chill in the air, and the amazing transformation of holiday booths in a winter wonderland.

Booths lined the snowy path, giant fire pits fully burning for the hot dogs and roasted marshmallows, holiday lights and garland on the glass wooden frames, with warmed temporary mini portable heaters in each portable booth. If the weather gets bad, the alternative plan is to move indoors- but as long as the weather holds with cold and limited snow, the portable glass wooden booths will be good.

—hand-knit scarves, homemade jams, crafts, jewelry, food, pastries, stickers, book club events, and so much more!

Floyd's apothecary booth shimmered under strands of golden lights. His hand-poured candles were lined neatly in rows—labels handwritten in his looping script: *Snowfall Serenity*, *Fireside Mint*, and *Cozy Nook Remedy*. The air around his stand smelled of vanilla, pine, and a faint note of citrus. Locals stopped just to inhale, book club guests cheered with delight. Many bought two or three candles at a time while Floyd explained the "scientific benefits of relaxation through scent" with his usual charming seriousness.

Just a few booths away, Poppy's pastry stand had stolen the show entirely. At its center stood a nine-tier holiday cake—a masterpiece of white frosting, sugared cranberries, edible flowers and pearls, with tiny marzipan cottages that looked just like Bean Hive Cottage itself. Visitors gasped and took photos as Poppy fussed proudly with the final touches. "It's the spirit of the season," she told Lucy. "A little sugar, a little magic, love, friends, and a whole lot of frosting to hold it all together."

Everyone laughed.

The jewelry-making booth was one of the busiest corners of the Bean Hive Cottage Holiday Market. Tables sparkled with trays of glass beads, pearls, charms, and tiny golden bells that jingled whenever someone reached for a new strand. There were so many great trinkets and options with creative opportunities, it was so hard to choose! Miss Betty even had music playing, as well as some theater members singing, while helping visitors with picking out charms and making their exquisite piece. Miss Betty had adorable ornaments that you could also make, some people chose to make both!

Guests from the book clubs mingled with townsfolk and tourists, stringing together bracelets and ornaments while sipping hot cocoa from paper cups. Lucy's idea of self-serve, free ready made cocoa stands was a huge hit.

The winter tour buses stopped, and everyone seemed excited to take the first photo at the Bean Hive Cottage photo op booth.

The chatter and laughter mixed with the faint sound of carolers, creating a melody that made the whole event feel alive.

Miss Betty, ever the multitasker, was in charge of the dance, theater, and jewelry operation. Her bangles jingled as she moved from table to table, offering advice on bead combinations and clasp techniques. "Now remember," she said dramatically, "if your bracelet doesn't sparkle from the stage, it's just not worth wearing!" She had set up a small sign-up table at the back, cleverly combining jewelry-making with registration forms for her theater, dance, and jewelry making classes. Her dancers and theater members did perform at different times during the event, everyone loved the amazing talent. She also owed the Miss Betty's Dance and Theater Store located inside her dance and theater studio. Miss Betty loved advertising her talents, and especially showing off those talents. The current members were doing skits, as well as dances at various times.

Visitors from nearby towns lined up to join, charmed by Miss Betty's flair and the promise of community. Many visitors had driven in, while others took the train or plane,- just to experience the Bean Hive Cottage holiday buzz they'd heard about.

Even the mayor stopped by to thread a few beads, claiming it was "excellent for stress management," though Miss Betty teased him mercilessly about his crooked pattern.

By afternoon, the tables were covered in glitter, ribbon, and laughter. Little girls wore their new bracelets proudly; older visitors compared necklaces and swapped stories about past winters in Bean Hive Town. Miss Betty stood back with a satisfied sigh. "We have more than jewelry today," she said, smiling. "We have memories—and maybe a few future performers too." Miss Betty smiled as she watched the sign up sheet for the seamstress club become completely full. The seamstress club was a group that helped with costume making for the theater, as well as learning how to sew and make things for charity events.

The first book-club retreat gathered in the parlor, their chatter and laughter blending with the popping of the fire. The parlor was a picture of warmth and nostalgia. A roaring fire filled the room with a golden glow, reflecting off shelves lined with well-loved novels and snow globe decorations. Plush armchairs circled the hearth, and the faint scent of orange peel and clove drifted from the simmer pot

Poppy had left on the mantle. Lucy moved quietly through the group, topping off teacups and smiling as the women debated which book best captured the spirit of the season.

At the heart of the discussion sat a woman named Margo, who insisted that *Little Women* was "the most perfect Christmas story ever written." Across from her, a younger guest countered with *The Christmas Train,* declaring that love and travel made a better holiday pairing than moral lessons and patchwork dresses. The laughter that followed filled every corner of the room, rising and falling like music. These small moments were the greatest of memories, and what continued to bring life and dreams to the cottage.

When Olive passed through to deliver a tray of shortbread and cinnamon tea, she paused to listen for a moment. "You all sound like the Gazette at deadline," she said with a grin. "Only with better snacks." The group erupted in giggles, and Lucy jotted a note in her organizer: *Next retreat—ask Olive to host a storytelling night. The parlor book club event was going very well, and Olive was primarily in charge of keeping up with the parlor functions. Lucy was running around everywhere, checking in on the book club guests, as well as capturing the news new article, and overseeing the Bean Hive Cottage Holiday Market.*

The second book club guests were settled in the sunroom, where the view through frosted windows and mugs of cocoa steamed beside stacks of novels. The sunroom glowed like a snow globe brought to life. Frosted windows framed the soft white world outside, where snowflakes drifted past the glass in lazy spirals. Inside, the air was filled with the scent of cocoa, cinnamon, and pine. A string of twinkle lights ran along the window ledge, catching the reflection of the mugs that steamed beside towers of novels stacked high on the table. Guests lounged on cozy chairs with plaid blankets over their laps, flipping pages and occasionally sighing contentedly.

Annie had taken her hostess duties seriously. She moved gracefully from chair to chair, refilling cocoa, straightening napkins, and offering Poppy's sugared scones on a tiered tray that looked almost too pretty to touch. Every so often, she would pause to join in a lively conversation about the book selection of the week, nodding thoughtfully before returning to her duties with a smile. It was clear Lucy trusted her completely—Annie had the calm, steady charm that kept the group running smoothly.

At one point, a guest spilled cocoa on her notebook, and Annie swooped in with a clean towel and an easy laugh. "No worries," she said, "Bean Hive Cottage stories always come with a little sweetness on the page." The group chuckled, and soon everyone was sharing stories about their own holiday reading mishaps—books dropped in bathtubs, book trading, dog-eared pages saved with candy wrappers, dreams, and half-read novels rediscovered every December.

Another guest brought magnetic bookmarks to the club, and everyone discussed how incredible it was. Most of the guests folded the book page as they read, or used paper bookmarks. The magnetic bookmarks were a hit of conversation.

The laughter and love of books, the joy of the season, and the amazing company.

When Lucy peeked in to check on them, she found the whole scene so peaceful that she didn't dare interrupt. The book club retreat, she thought, had found its own kind of holiday magic. Lucy loved books, loved reading, and her absolute favorite thing in the whole wide world was to see others joy from reading.

The third book club just down the hall occupied the library, lost in quiet reading and soft music. The library was a world of its own—a sanctuary of quiet elegance tucked deep inside Bean Hive Cottage. Shelves of dark walnut gleamed under the soft glow of brass sconces, and the grand fireplace crackled steadily beneath a marble mantle adorned with evergreen garlands and flickering candles.

The scent of old paper mixed with wood polish and pine, creating an air of nostalgia that made guests instinctively lower their voices to a reverent hush.

Michaelangelo, ever the attentive host, moved through the room with practiced ease.

He wore a perfectly pressed vest and carried a silver tray of tea cups balanced with impossible precision. Every time a guest reached for an empty mug, he appeared as if by magic—refilling drinks, replenishing pastries, and ensuring the group had everything they needed.

"A well-fed reader," he liked to say, "is far less likely to stage a literary revolt."

That quote proved timely, because a minor dispute had just broken out near the corner window. Two guests had their hearts set on the same overstuffed armchair—the one closest to the fire with the best view of the snow. Voices rose briefly, but Michaelangelo stepped in with charm and diplomacy, offering a compromise: one could take the seat for the morning session, the other after lunch. Both parties agreed, and soon the tension melted as quickly as snow on a warm hearth.

The comfortable seating, the pillows, the quilts, the soft throws, and the charm of Bean Hive Cottage Inn, always brought such magic to guests near and far. The tattered granny throw blankets, seemed to always sell out before the book clubs even begin. Sure guests may use the comforts of the cottage amenities, however to buy and own a Bean Hive Cottage Tattered granny throw blanket was highly sought after. This room has been a favorite to many guests, and has the best display of the tattered granny throw blankets for sale.

The group eventually settled into their rhythm, though not without lively debate. The novel they'd chosen—a sweeping historical romance—had divided the room.

One guest found the protagonist "too dramatic for her own good," while another argued she was "a woman ahead of her time." The discussion grew so passionate that Michaelangelo later claimed he could hear it echoing through the hall like courtroom proceedings.

By dusk, the library had regained its calm. Guests sat curled in armchairs, the last rays of light painting the walls amber. Michaelangelo dimmed the sconces and put on a soft instrumental record that hummed through the stillness. The flicker of the fire, the rustle of pages, and the quiet murmurs of contentment made it feel like a secret world hidden from the storm outside—a warm, book-scented refuge that could only exist in Bean Hive Cottage.

The fourth book club group took over the loft, transformed into a twinkling hideaway filled with bean bags, super soft chairs, quilts and charm. This room is rarely used unless there is overflow at the Inn. This year's Bean Hive Cottage Market was in full swing and more inquiries than space available for the book club events.

Murder Mystery in the Loft, sounded like a book itself! The upstairs loft, which had been transformed into a twinkling, magical hideaway, was so cozy and cute with giant quilts, old time lanterns, a filled snack station, crackling fireplace, stained glass windows, and the incredible wooden walnut decor. Perfect for a Murder Mystery group. Soft golden lights draped across wooden beams, while the candle-like lanterns flickered from every corner.

The room shimmered with a mysterious glow, perfect for the evening's theme—a live-action murder mystery luncheon. A large round table was set in the center, surrounded by elegant mismatched chairs, each with a name card hinting at the guest's character role. This room offered such space for games, murder mystery activities, as well as reading. The excitement in the air was thick with curiosity and laughter as everyone prepared to play their part. Not only would they explore lunch and dinner and overnight about their favorite mysteries, they would act out a mystery book scene.

Miss Betty even had a cart with costumes she brought over earlier, to make the entire day a true mystery theater live action event. There was even a fun social media photo opportunity, where everyone has a chance to pose and post.

This particular group was known around Bean Hive Cottage as the "Mystery Buffs." They thrived on suspense, secrets, and dramatic flair. They were always watching the news, and questioning everything in current events. This group always has a story to tell, regardless of current events or past scandals, they know it all.

Today's story involved a missing heirloom, a secret passage, and a mysterious thud from the next room. Guests eagerly clutched their clue cards, whispering theories before the first course even arrived.

The sound of rustling papers and half-suppressed laughter filled the loft, blending perfectly with the cozy crackle of the fireplace below.

Michaelangelo, ever the gracious host, oversaw the event with calm precision and good humor. He made sure everyone received their meals promptly, that no one missed a clue, and that the servers moved smoothly between tables without disrupting the play. His quick wit and patient smile helped guide the group through moments of confusion—especially when debates broke out about the weapon of choice. "What do you mean it was the axe?" one guest exclaimed. "I thought it was the knife!" Another chimed in, "The clues don't match! The door wasn't even locked!"

The room erupted with good-natured chaos. Between bites of their luncheon, the guests argued, laughed, and speculated wildly about the culprit.

Someone swore they heard a knock followed by a faint thud upstairs; others insisted it was part of the story. The air was alive with mystery and mirth, and the laughter echoed down the stairwell into the main parlor below. Even the staff paused now and then to grin at the animated chatter coming from the loft.

By the end of the luncheon, the murder had been "solved," though not without a few friendly disputes about who really should've been the guilty party. Michaelangelo congratulated the group with a playful bow, declaring them the most spirited guests of the weekend. The Bean Hive Cottage staff cleared the tables with quiet efficiency, still smiling at the echoes of laughter that lingered in the loft. The fourth book club's lively mystery afternoon would be remembered as one of the most entertaining gatherings of the season. By Evening they were able to explore another enchanted mystery of fun and engagement.

And the fifth book club group had claimed the conservatory, surrounded by winter plants and the smell of Poppy's spiced cider. The view was impressive, and the guests all brought gifts for their book club gift exchange.

The romance readers immediately began teasing one another about which characters would most likely sneak a kiss behind the towering ferns. The ferns were huge, and looked magnificent with red garland and popcorn strands draped around them.

Someone joked that the ivy creeping up the wall probably knew more about dramatic love triangles than any of them ever would. Everyone laughed.

Another guest mentioned the incredible wallpaper trim on the one wall, and how romantic the room actually was with the glass modern windows. While another guest joked that the wallpaper trim was preserved before this new addition to the Inn was added, making it a fond old and new blend. Next thing everyone was talking about romance and interior design.

Laughter echoed through the glass room as they compared their favorite swoon-worthy scenes to the "overly clingy" vines and "mysterious, brooding" winter blooms.

Dr. Lu and Mrs. Lu arrived carrying trays of heart-shaped sugar cookies. Juniper, bright-eyed and rosy-cheeked, skipped behind them with a basket of poinsettias.

'Holiday health for everyone!' Dr. Lu announced proudly, handing out cookies. Dr. Lu then handed

Floyd a cookie. 'Eat one and you'll feel better about your cholesterol.'

'Or worse about your willpower,' Floyd said, taking two. Dr. Lu also brought a big bag of mini emergency first aid kits, and handed them to Michaelangelo. "We must always be prepared".

Michaelangelo smiled and set the kits up on the counter, just in case. He knew that Dr. Lu couldn't go anywhere without some type of medical kit.

Moira, Lucy's mother, swept into the cottage like a blizzard in pearls. Her fur shimmered, and her perfume arrived a full second before she did.

'Darling, where's the tea set?' she asked. 'The High Tea and Low Gossip Charity reunion begins promptly at three.'

'In the dining room,' Lucy said patiently. 'And yes, we polished the silver.'

'Excellent,' Moira said, gliding off. 'A century of charity gossip deserves sparkle.'

The High Tea & Low Gossip Charity, guests arrived in a flurry of elegant coats and feather-trimmed hats, each one balancing a delicate gift box for the charity raffle and a teacup they insisted on bringing "for the aesthetic." The dining room transformed into a scene straight from an old-world painting—lace tablecloths, towering tiered trays filled with pastries, and the faint clink of fine China.

Conversations bloomed almost instantly as everyone settled in, discussing everything from winter galas to who had switched salad forks with dessert forks at last year's luncheon.

Moira presided over the gathering like a seasoned empress of etiquette, ensuring every guest had tea in hand before launching into the reunion's traditions. "Remember, ladies," she announced with theatrical flourish, "we practice *low gossip*, which means we only whisper the truth quietly." A ripple of laughter swept through the room. The women leaned closer to one another, delighted to toe the line between dignity and indulgence as they shared their most refined tidbits of news.

Soon, the topics shifted to high-society dilemmas: the debate over which charity should host the winter auction, the scandal of someone wearing ivory instead of winter white, and the whispered rumor of an unexpected romance between two long-time committee rivals. Every revelation was delivered in hushed tones with dramatic pauses, as if the walls could talk.

Lucy drifted between tables, refilling teapots and nibbling on lemon scones, amused by how seriously everyone took the art of delicate conversation.

At the center of the room, Moira unveiled her signature "Conversation Cards," which she claimed encouraged sophisticated discussions but usually led to mild chaos. Questions ranged from "Which virtue would you embroider on a handkerchief?" to "If love were a pastry, which would it be?" The answers sparked animated chatter—some sentimental, some outrageous.

One guest declared love was a cream puff: beautiful, messy, and irresistible. Another insisted it was a scone—simple, dependable, and best served warm.

By the end of the afternoon, the tea had grown cold, but the room buzzed with satisfied chatter. The charity pledges were generous, the pastries devoured, and the low gossip had been—by all accounts—elevated to an art form. Moira clasped her hands in triumph, certain the event had been a grand success. Lucy simply smiled, grateful that in Bean Hive Cottage, even high society came with a touch of humor and a whole lot of heart.

Suddenly one of the guests looked outside the window and remarked, "what beautiful dancers." Then everyone gathered at the window to see.

Miss Betty was outside with holiday dancers on the front lawn for the winter recital practicing. She waved her yellow feather like a conductor's baton.

'And twirl! And lift! No one sprain anything before showtime!' she shouted as snowflakes landed on her eyelashes.

Dr. Lu walked by smiling.

Marvin grumbled as he tried to keep the hot dogs stocked at the firepits. Floyd was watching Marvin, while holding a mug of coffee and offering unhelpful advice.

'That one's burnt.'

'You're burnt, it's a hot dog, it doesn't matter,' Marvin shot back. 'At least the hot dogs are well done.'

Floyd then asked Marvin why he is always the one on hot dog duty?

Marvin let out a long sigh, poking at the firepit with the tongs as Floyd continued his commentary from the safety of his coffee mug.

"Maybe rotate them clockwise," Floyd suggested, absolutely certain he was being helpful. Marvin stared at him, deadpan. "Rotate *yourself* clockwise right back to the cider stand," he muttered, but Floyd stayed put, grinning like he'd just improved the entire operation.

A gust of wind sent snow swirling across the path, and Marvin's hot dog tray nearly went flying. Floyd reached out one lazy hand—still holding his mug—and steadied it just in time. "See? I'm basically your assistant," he declared proudly. "You're basically a menace," Marvin replied, grabbing another package of hot dogs and tossing it onto the counter. "And if you're my assistant, you're fired."

Before Floyd could respond, Miss Betty appeared out of nowhere, bundled in a gigantic purple scarf that fluttered behind her like a parade banner. "Marvin, darling, I need twelve hot dogs immediately! The tap dancers are starving, and I can't have them fainting mid–snow shuffle." Marvin blinked. "Miss Betty, this is not a catering express lane—this is a firepit." But she was already gone, shouting encouragement to an invisible chorus line.

Just then the mailman, who had finally made it down the icy path after three near catastrophes, called over to them. "Marvin! I've delivered mail through hurricanes, but this path is a lawsuit waiting to happen. We need salt. Lots of salt." Marvin opened his mouth to respond, but Floyd beat him to it. "Add that to Marvin's list! He's very organized." Marvin simply closed his eyes and counted to five.

Just then, Lucy arrived with a tray of steaming cocoa, handing one to Marvin before he could protest. "You look like you're about to throw a hot dog at someone," she said gently. "I might," Marvin admitted. "But I'll aim carefully." Floyd raised his mug in toast. "To Marvin—the hottest hot-dogger in Bean Hive Cottage!" Marvin rolled his eyes, but even he couldn't help the small smile tugging at the corner of his mouth as snowflakes drifted down around them.

Down by the path, the mailman from the post office was slipping on the ice again, clutching his mailbag. 'We need salt, not garlands!' he yelled.

Miss Betty just waved cheerfully. 'Merry Christmas! Try not to sue the town this year!'

The scent of roasting chestnuts from a nearby vendor drifted through the market. Children's laughter mixed with carolers singing by the gazebo.

Poppy's pastry table drew a crowd—gingerbread loaves, apple turnovers, and snowflake cookies glittering with sugar. 'We're out of scones again!' she called. 'Floyd, stop flirting and fetch more trays!'

Floyd raised his hands in mock surrender. 'Yes, ma'am. But I'm charging overtime for pie slices.'

Inside, The High Tea and Low Gossip Society gathered, dressed in lace and pearls. Crystal glasses chimed as Moira toasted 'to a hundred years of tasteful talk.'

Olive leaned over to Lucy and whispered, 'Tasteful's a stretch.'

'Don't let her hear you,' Lucy whispered back. 'She'll add you to the gossip minutes.'

Outside, the sky blushed pink as lanterns lit across the market.

Marvin finished the last of the fire roasted hot dogs, and opened up one last back of marshmallows for smores.

Lucy smiled, today was like a storybook illustration.

Miss Betty's dancers twirled through delicate snow while Juniper and the theater students threw handfuls of glitter that sparkled in the lamplight.

Dr. Lu announced that he was available for free blood-pressure checks 'between cocoa tastings.'

Mrs. Lu rolled her eyes but smiled. 'At least you'll meet half the town.'

Annie paused on the porch, heart full. Around her, laughter spilled through the windows, and the music from the gazebo drifted softly across the snow. What a great day this has been. Lucy joined, and gave her a hug.

Moira approached, linking arms with her daughter and grand-daughter. 'You've made

quite a name for yourself, Lucy. Bean Hive Cottages never looked so beautiful.'

'It's not just me,' Lucy said, watching Poppy carry another tray outside. 'It's all of us.'

'Even Marvin?' Moira teased. 'Especially Marvin,' Lucy said with a grin. 'He's the glue—and the gossip.'

The bell tower struck eight, echoing over the rooftops. The lights shimmered brighter, and the crowd gathered for the evening carol.

Together they sang beneath the softly falling snow—neighbors, friends, and visitors—each note blending into the next until the

The whole town seemed to hum with warmth.

When the last song ended and the lanterns flickered low, Lucy looked around at Bean Hive Cottage glowing in the night. It wasn't just a building—it was a heartbeat, pulsing with laughter, love, and the unshakable magic of the holidays.

Chapter 13

SAVE THE DAM

Through the trees at first Lucy thought it was ice shifting, but then she heard it clearly: The storm hit Bean Hive Cottage like a snow tsunami—loud, dramatic, and full of complaints. Twelve straight hours of wet, heavy snow buried the town under a frosting layer that Poppy would later call "beautiful if you were inside, catastrophic if you were out shoveling it." She had a love hate relationship with the snow, depending on delivery or baking days.

But the real trouble began the next morning when Pinehaven Road collapsed in a perfect, postcard-unworthy heap of slush, broken asphalt, and the unmistakable roar of rushing water. Yes, it was a terrible night, a terrible severe storm that brought historic rain and snow mixed levels or devastation to the town. The deluge occurred about 1am in the morning, Bean Hive time. Sadly when the catastrophic event occurred, the old Bean Hive Grist Mill broke away and was pulled across the bridge and roadway. The collapse not only created awful damage on the bridge and roadway; it created a completely destroyed Bean Hive Harbor Pond ecosystem and park area. The pond was drained completely by the wreckage, and also causing those Bean Hive residents struggles to get to the town. You see the bridge and roadway now was no longer the main local thoroughfare-it was shut off.

Residents now had to drive all the way around, backroads not designed for heavy traffic, and cross two railroad tracks to get to Bean Hive for shopping, medical, or any town needs. Sadly the aquatic habitat, and the area wildlife, were devastated with some animals being relocated, others rehabilitated at the Bean Hive Wildlife Rescue and Sanctuary. Even local residents were putting food and shelter outside for the animals displaced.

Mayor Ooglemyer has been devastated, reporting that the Bean Hive Medical Response team is now delayed 7 to 10 minutes longer due to the incident.

The Bean Hive Grist Mill Pond dam, a humble structure built back when people wore suspenders, and used horse drawn carriages, had finally cracked under the pressure of the storm. A gash along the side sent water spilling into the marsh, down the hill, flooding areas that were normally dry, and flooding the marina. The pressure also flooded homes, basements, and straight toward the quiet stretch of Pinehaven—taking trees, an old mailbox, and unfortunately, Marvin's cardboard Elvis with it. Sadly the road, bridge and Bean Hive Grist Mill were not able to hold on. With everything wiped out, it looked like a collapsed, unconnected mess. The area appeared unrecognizable.

The next few mornings after the horrible storm, Bean Hive Cottage felt like a small town halfway between a Hallmark postcard and a panic attack from the apocalypse. Town members were walking around, almost like a scene right out of a zombie movie, almost as if in a trance.

The town was awake, the High Tea and Low Gossip ladies charity, were all at Marvin's discussing how they would help rebuild. Moira was trying to keep everyone calm when the ladies had a bit of a scuffle as to bake sales vs. raffle tickets.

Mayor Ooglemyer stood in the middle of Marvin's Diner, rubbing his temples. "This is my worst nightmare, we need to fix this," he muttered.

Marvin stepped forward, "we'll fix it, definitely not tomorrow or the next day, but we will."

Moira smiled, "the High Tea and Low Gossip ladies and I are already working on baking brownies, putting up posters, opening up a raffle, my husband will step in with the bank and see what options the town has."

Mayor Ooglemyer began to smile, "thank you, thank you, we will make a bigger, sturdier dam, a dam that will be unbreakable, with...maybe titanium or is titanium even a thing?"

The diner was full of conversation, and fundraising ideas. Everyone was wanting to help pitch in and Mayor Ooglemyer, already had the town crew out working.

Michelangelo stopped in, dripping wet mud, snow, rainwater all dripping off of him. Everyone watched as he stood in Marvin's doorway, almost as if everyone was too overwhelmed to speak.

Marvin says, "okay if no one is going to say it, I will say it, what the hell happened to you?"

Michelangelo looked exhausted, and frustrated, "I had to drive all the way around, the bridge and road was washed out and I'm dripping wet as my house is flooded from the weather. My jeep was stuck in the mud, as the driveway was flooded in mud, and I had to take the shovel to scoop the mud. Lucky for me, I had chains already on the tires due to recent off roading projects. Part of half pine creek is completely mud and debris. I finally was able to get out, but not without getting a little dirty."

"A little dirty, how about a lot dirty. Oh, no, if you got flooded all the way out there, that means others did too; that sounds terrible," Moira exclaimed.

Michelangelo, trying to wipe off the mud and clean himself up with a towel Marvin handed him. "Yes, the flooding spread all the way across, reaching the north east end of Bean Hive."

Mayor Ooglemyer sat beside Michaelangelo, and the two began to discuss the road issues, the weather issues and frustrations with what to do.

Marvin kept the coffee hot and the communication lively. Moira and the High Tea and Low Gossip ladies got to work, to save the dam. Signs were going up everywhere, and phone calls were being made. She was able to get a website set up, along with the local radio station.

Miss Betty stood outside the Bean Hive Post Office taping up yet another homemade sign:

"SAVE THE DAM — DANCE FUNDRAISER COMING SOON!"
"SAVE THE DAM-BAKE SALE COMING SOON!"

Moira smiled, "thank you Miss Betty, we are all a team and we can do it."

Miss Betty smiled back and the next thing you know, her dance students began cheering, "go go go, fight fight fight, save the dam, save the dam, go go go, fight fight fight, save the dam!"

Floyd was walking by and suddenly squinted up at the sign.

"You spelled 'fundraiser' wrong, Miss Betty."

She huffed. "I'm a dance and drama teacher, not a spelling teacher, how do you expect me to know how to spell, Floyd. People should be impressed that I'm spelling anything at all. Besides this adds character development to the cause."

Floyd smiled, "just letting you know that is all, keep up the good work."

Miss Betty smirked, "right back at ya Floyd."

Across the street, Marvin was dragging folding tables from the diner to the sidewalk yet again, because he couldn't decide between a Cars With Coffee theme or a Cars and Pancakes theme. He was outside measuring and taking photos with his phone.

"Marvin," Lucy called out, walking by with a notebook tucked under her arm, "you're going to freeze in this drizzle, why are you messing around outside with a table."

"I am fueled by purpose," Marvin declared dramatically. "And possibly three espressos. I know we gotta save the dam but I have other tasks to prepare for."

Lucy smirked, "right now, you mean right now in the middle of this weather and a catastrophic event to the town, you are working on a task? I'm sorry but the only task we all need to be working on is saving the dam."

Michelangelo trotted behind Marvin with a bottle labeled—

"Floyd's Citrus Moonbeam Car Glow — TEST BATCH."

"Floyd said we shouldn't shake this too hard. Or drink it. This will be awesome for the cars and whatever you decide theme"

Lucy blinked. "Drink it?! I would be very careful about anything Floyd says is going to glow. You drink that, and you might be glowing in the sunlight"

Michelangelo shrugged. "He said someone always tries."

Marvin smiled, "I'm thinking here, I'm thinking here, if we serve pancakes or not; I have time to decide on the exact theme this year, I just want the measurements down."

Michelangelo chimed in, "how about we set up a poll at the diner and let the town decide the theme? Cars with coffee or pancakes or both?"

Marvin smiled, "perfect, you make the sign and let the town know."

Marina Meltdown OMG

Down by the marina, a line of townsfolk stood staring at the water like it had personally offended them.

The storm had caused the water level to rise and spill over in odd directions, and the docks bobbed with an unsettling wobble. OMG the Marina Meltdown has happened. Mayor Ooglemyer was all upset, and the town residents that lived on the marina were not happy at all with the sudden influx of water spilling everywhere. This plus the roadway and bridge that was no longer, creating more traffic by the marina. The marina had damage, wind damage and excess flooding damage due to the dam breaking.

Poppy walked over by the marina to look at what all the Bean Hive buzz was about.

Poppy wrapped her pink scarf tighter around her neck. The wind was chilly and cold, with a bit of dampness in the air.

"If we can't do Strawberry Sail this spring, I swear I'll—"

"What? Bake harder?" Lucy teased. Lucy was taking notes for the newsletter and the gazette. News 21 was on their way, and Lucy wanted to get prime interview scoops before they arrived.

"YES," Poppy said. "WITH PASSION."

Poppy smiled and gave Lucy a big hug.

Her boots crunched as she walked closer to the edge. The ferry sign hung crooked, the wooden beams still slick from overflow. The idea that the marina might not open next season made the whole town feel... off. Like Christmas lights with one rogue bulb.

Captain Stedman, who ran the spring ferry to the Sound, frowned into the icy wind.

"If that dam sends another surge, these docks won't see April. The marina is toast! We have the boats all in the the dry stack facilities or the boat yard, this has been a tragedy to the town and the marina"

The worry spread as fast as the winter cold:

What would happen to tourism?

The pedal-boats, the kayaks?

The summer boat camp?

The boat tours?

The swim club summer events?

The Summer Picnic on a boat gala?

Everyone began to buzz with conversation and dismay, what will happen and what will be done to fix this disastrous tragedy. More questions continued....

What is going to happen....

To the fishing season?

To the spring regatta?

To Floyd's Maritime Aromatherapy Workshop ("The Sea Within — Guided by Scent")?

Everything in Bean Hive connected to everything else. Break one thread, and the whole web trembled.

Lucy scribbled notes furiously.

This was her book now: not just a fundraiser, but a love letter to a town held together by coffee, chaos, and pure determination.

Just then, Lucy felt her phone buzz in her pocket. Another town-wide alert...

Urgent, urgent read immediately,

from Mayor Ooglemyer—well, technically from his assistant, because the mayor still hadn't figured out how to send a group text without accidentally attaching a selfie.

ALERT: "Town Hall Meeting at 6 PM. Emergency Dam Discussion. Bring positivity. And possibly towels."

Lucy groaned. Towels? That couldn't be good.

As she tucked her phone away, a blast of frigid air whipped through the marina, rattling the crooked ferry sign so hard it clanged like a warning bell. The sound echoed across the grey water, reminding her just how fragile everything felt right now. She bent down to touch the ground, the mud caked in the earth with rubble. This is not Bean Hive. This looks like Armageddon.

Behind her, Miss. Betty appeared, bundled in three scarves and the kind of determination only an impromptu drama teacher possessed.

"Lucy! Have you heard the news? I'm forming a committee. A real one. With clipboards."

"Oh no," Lucy said. "What kind of committee?"

"A Save the Dam morale committee. We need spirit. We need unity. We need—"

"—glitter?" Lucy guessed.

"Absolutely not," Miss. Betty huffed. "This is a serious matter. We'll use metallic confetti. Much more dignified."

Before Lucy could respond, Miss. Betty leaned closer, lowering her voice conspiratorially.

"We may also need a fundraiser," she whispered. "Perhaps... a themed dance? I'm thinking 'Shake Your Dam Tail', but I'm open to revisions."

Lucy winced. "Maybe... maybe let's put a pin in the name."

But she couldn't help smiling. Leave it to Bean Hive the town with heart—when infrastructure threatened to collapse, the residents responded with pastries, clipboards, and questionable dance themes. Lucy felt it was up to her to get the news out there, to livestream, to post on social media, to share everywhere. Bean Hive needed help, and needed help quickly.

Miss. Betty walked around, smiled at Lucy, and began dancing in the cold misty wind. "Nothing will get Bean Hive down, oh no, oh no, no, no, nothing."

And yet... beneath the humor, a knot tightened in Lucy's chest. The worry, the challenges of her own life, the book club, the town, the entire Bean Hive Ecosystem. What is this little East Coast Long Island town going to do, surrounded on one side is the Atlantic ocean, the other is the Long Island Sound, and then the dam breaks. Not to mention water is dripping cold from the sky.

Water, water, everywhere. She even felt a teardrop, dripping down her cheek. "I have water within me and outside of me."

If the marina didn't open, if the dam kept surging, if the county kept shrugging—what then? What happened to a town whose charm depended on water, ferries, festivals, and traditions older than the Bean Hive Grist Mill?

What happened to my home?

Lucy took a steadying breath, staring out at the frost-rimmed docks. Whatever came next, one thing was certain:

This wasn't just a town problem. This was a community problem.

It was her problem too.

And if Bean Hive was going to survive this winter, they were going to have to fight for it—together. The entire town would have to be all in, to make the effort and build back what was lost.

By six o'clock, Town Hall buzzed like a beehive on espresso. Folding chairs scraped, winter coats rustled, and the scent of Poppy's emergency cinnamon muffins wafted through the room like a calming agent nobody was actually calm enough to appreciate.

Lucy slipped into a seat near the front just as Mayor Ooglemyer shuffled to the podium, carrying twelve disorganized papers and the emotional energy of a man who'd aged five years since breakfast.

He was shaking and asked Lucy if she would clean his fogged glasses. He finally adjusted himself and began the meeting.

Mayor Ooglemyer stood at the podium, tapping the microphone, tapping it, "testing, testing."

He cleared his throat three times, dramatically before speaking again.

"Good evening, residents of Bean Hive. I hereby call this emergency meeting of the Village Town, Bean Hive Village Town Council to order." He quickly adjusted his glasses, and nodded to the secretary to begin to take notes. He tried to appear authoritative despite his favorite cinnamon treats that Poppy brought and set up in the back of the room.

A loud boom crackled from the speakers.

"Okay, it works," yelled Floyd, who was in charge of the speakers.

"Alright, everyone, if we could—"

A chair screeched loudly.

"If we could please—"

Another chair screeched. Screeeeechhhhh... Screeeeechhhhh....

"—STOP SCRAPING THE CHAIRS!"

Silence.

The mayor cleared his throat again. "As you know, the dam overflowed again last night. Ugh... The surge reached the marina and—well—Captain Stedman is convinced the docks are 'toast.' His word, not mine."

Sniffling was heard in the crowd.

Captain Stedman stood, arms crossed. He was wearing his Captain uniform, and refused to sit. He appeared angry, yet nervous all at the same time.

"I said charred brioche, actually."

"Right," the mayor sighed. "Charmed brioche. Fine."

A wave of murmurs rolled through the crowd.

Miss. Betty shot up from her seat, scarf flapping like a victory banner. She always appeared dramatic, no matter the event.

"We need organization! A plan! A unified mission! And clipboards—I brought clipboards."

Everyone watching in disbelief, unsure of how or what to do.

"Betty, please sit," the mayor said, but too late—she was already passing them out like communion wafers.

Lucy whispered to her, "You're starting a movement, aren't you?"

Miss. Betty smiled. "Honey, I've been waiting my whole life." Betty was walking around, passing out the clipboards for sign up, while her scarf drew much attention. You see Miss. Betty always had a way with not just communication but fashion, she was always dressed for any and all occasions. One thing the village could count on was her knack for design. One day she is wearing her tippy shoes and the next war zone boots.

The mayor continued, "The county claims that because Bean Hive Cottage is incorporated village—"

Groans erupted.

"—they are not responsible for funding dam repairs."

Oh nooo, oh nooo the town members were gasping for air. Everyone was sitting in shock.

A collective cry sounded. Someone yelled, "WHAT DO WE PAY TAXES FOR THEN?!"

Another person shouted, "NOTHING! THAT'S THE TRICK!"

A few other members were talking about the frustration of not feeling like the county cared or the people even mattered.

Poppy, holding a tray of muffins, chimed in innocently:

"Does anyone need a snack before we riot?" "We all need to keep our strength up and create a plan, this can not be happening, sometimes bad things happen but we are strong and we will survive. I have more muffins, cookies, and a daily slice of food comfort at the bakery to keep us all going strong." Everyone looked, smiled and grabbed a snack.

Moira glided to her feet, perfectly coiffed despite the cold. She then began to straighten up her posture and button a button on her navy jacket.

"I would simply like to announce that I will be hosting a High Tea and Low Gossip event, for High Tension Stress, this Sunday to raise funds. Scones, gossip, and—if necessary—emergency breathwork."

Someone clapped. Then another member clapped, then the whole room began to clap.

Someone else muttered, "Of course she is."

Mayor Ooglemyer rubbed his eyes and sniffled with a small teardrop, you could tell he was really emotional.

"Look, folks, until the county cooperates, we need ideas. Realistic ones."

Mrs. Lu and Dr. Lu brought medical safety supplies, kids water bottles and bags of paper goods.

Captain Stedman bellowed, "Close the ferry?"

Half the room gasped like he'd suggested canceling Christmas.

"WITHOUT THE FERRY, WE DIE!" shouted Old Man Riggins dramatically.

"We won't die," Lucy said, standing slowly.

The room fell quiet.

"But we will lose what makes this town us."

Her voice steadied.

"The marina, the ferry, the spring regatta, the workshops, the summer picnic on the boat event, the shops by the water—everything depends on that dam holding. If the county won't help, then we need to show them

we're not some sleepy little village town they can ignore. We're Bean Hive Village Town. We fight with muffins, meetings, and questionable dance themes."

Miss. Betty perked. "I KNEW YOU LIKED THE DANCE IDEA!"

Lucy continued, "We need a plan. A fundraiser. A petition. Pressure on the county. And—yes—maybe a badly named dance."

The room burst into applause—messy, loud, overlapping applause that sounded like hope.

The mayor straightened, suddenly looking a little taller.

"Alright then. Committee volunteers?"

Every hand shot up.

Well... except Old Man Riggins, who whispered, "I'm too old for clipboards," but raised his hand anyway.

Lucy smiled.

The fight for the dam had officially begun.

Mayor Ooglemyer smiled, "alright, everyone, I know we are all scared, tired, cold, but we have a dam to save and a dam to save we will save."

Meanwhile, Mayor Ooglemyer locked himself in his office after the meeting, claiming he needed "a moment of quiet reflection."

According to the town clerk, he spent that moment:

reorganizing the pencils by height

sobbing into a box of tissues labeled "Emergency Emotional Supplies"

and writing an angry letter to the county that began,

"To Whom It May Concern (and apparently does NOT care)"

Lucy knocked gently on the door.

"Mayor? We're planning a fundraiser schedule. Are you coming out?"

A long sniff.

"No."

"You have to approve the permits."

Another sniff.

"There are... so many permits."

Lucy leaned against the door.

"We're all in this together. Even Floyd. He said he'll bring the wax that may or may not explode."

The door cracked open an inch.

"How likely is... may?"

Lucy hesitated. "Unsure."

Mayor Ooglemyer wiped his eyes. "Fine. Fine! I'll come out. But no one gets to yell at me today."

He opened the door fully, eyes wild, hair sticking up like he'd been electrocuted.

"Not one yelling!" he repeated.

Michelangelo, standing nearby with a permit request in hand, whispered to Lucy,

"He's definitely getting yelled at today."

Lucy smiled, "thank you."

Next Day Fundraiser Frenzy

Within 24 hours, Bean Hive Cottage turned into a flurry of preparation.

Poppy's Bakery

Loaded with brainstorming: Dam Cookies

Dam Good Brownies

Save-the-Dam Scones

And a wildly popular idea: "The Dam Cupcake" — filled with surprise raspberry sauce.

("It gushes! Very thematic!" Poppy said, beaming.)

Marvin's Diner

Marvin created a themed drink:

"Storm Surge Latte."

He swore the foam "naturally" formed a wave shape.

Lucy suspected Michelangelo was carving the shapes with a spoon.

Floyd's Apothecary

Floyd, inspired by chaos, crafted:

"Emotional Support Snowstorm Oil"

"Dam Blockage Relief Tea"

and an herbal car wax that smelled suspiciously like holiday potpourri.

He also insisted on building a booth for the fundraiser shaped like a tiny dam, complete with trickling essential-oil-infused water.

Miss Betty

Miss Betty had turned the Town Hall basement into a dance-planning war room.

Glitter everywhere.

Posters everywhere.

A disco ball the size of a pumpkin.

She pointed at Lucy as soon as she entered.

"We need a raffle prize. Something that screams Bean Hive!"

"My book," Lucy said without hesitation.

Miss Betty clasped her hands dramatically.

"Autographed?"

"Of course."

"With a bookmark?"

"I can make one."

"With ribbon?"

"...sure."

"With glitter?"

"No."

Miss Betty gasped. "Heartless."

Even the Teens Got Involved

The Bean Hive High School seniors offered to run a social media campaign:

#SaveTheDamChallenge

in which you were supposed to film yourself standing dramatically near a frozen pond while delivering your best "We will rebuild!" speech.

It went locally viral within 4 hours.

But the Crisis Isn't Over...

As preparations took shape and the town hummed with chaotic optimism, the weather report flashed across every screen in Bean Hive:

ANOTHER COASTAL STORM EXPECTED IN 48 HOURS. FLOOD ADVISORY REMAINS IN EFFECT.

Lucy's stomach sank.

If the dam gave out any further...

If the east entrance was washed out entirely...

If the pond overflowed again...

The fundraiser wouldn't be enough.

Town Hall had never smelled so strongly of cinnamon, desperation, and hot glue. Miss Betty had officially transformed the room into something between a barn dance and a 1970s disco revival. Streamers hung from the ceiling like festive seaweed. The handmade banner stretched across the stage read:

SAVE THE DAM!

(A DANCE TO REMEMBER... OR FORGET, DEPENDING ON HOW IT GOES)

Lucy stepped in and stopped mid-stride.

"Wow," she whispered. "It looks like Pinterest threw up."

The morning the repairs were scheduled to begin, Bean Hive woke to a sky the color of pale honey — the kind of golden winter light that made even the cold feel hopeful. Snow still clung to the edges of Pinehaven Road, but there was finally a clear path to the damaged dam.

Lucy wrapped her scarf tighter around her neck as she stepped onto the ridge overlooking the pond. The workers from the county stood shoulder-to-shoulder with villagers from Bean Hive, and for the first time in weeks, no one looked angry.

They looked determined.

Mayor Ooglemyer strutted forward wearing a neon orange safety vest two sizes too big.

"Today," he declared, "we will rebuild the dam… and my reputation."

Michelangelo whispered, "One of those is more important, but I'll never say which."

The First Hammer Strike

A construction crew chief named Pete lifted a hammer, looked to the mayor for a dramatic cue, and the mayor nodded vigorously.

Pete struck the first beam with a satisfying crack.

The crowd burst into applause.

Poppy cried. "It's happening! It's really happening!"

Floyd dabbed his eyes with a handkerchief that smelled strongly of eucalyptus.

"It's not the dust," he insisted. "It's the… collective healing of structural integrity."

Lucy felt her throat tighten.

For weeks she had watched fear creep into her neighbors' eyes — fear for wildlife, for the marina, for their small-town identity. But this morning, the fear melted like frost under sunlight.

Community Labor, Bean Hive Style

The reconstruction became a town-wide event:

Poppy *set up a "Rebuild Refreshments" table with hot cocoa topped with cinnamon and tiny marshmallows shaped like beavers.*

Marvin *grilled breakfast sandwiches on a portable griddle, offering each worker a free "Dam Strong Sandwich."*

Floyd *gave everyone complimentary "Muscle Relief Herbal Balms" (which smelled like lavender mixed with assertiveness).*

Miss Betty *organized a cheer squad of retirees who clapped enthusiastically every time a beam was placed correctly.*

The high schoolers *livestreamed updates under the hashtag **#RebuildTheDam** which instantly blew up across Long Island.*

Even Captain Stedman stood by, arms crossed, nodding at every progress marker as if personally approving each log.

The workers loved the attention.

One of them joked, "I've rebuilt half the county and never once had a cheering section or pastries."

Poppy proudly puffed up at that.

"Well, this is Bean Hive. We don't just rebuild — we celebrate while doing it."

Everyone smiled, even the News 21 was there to capture the happenings.

Lucy found herself wandering closer to the waterline, watching the carp swim lazily below the ice. The sound of hammers, the laughter, the smell of cocoa — it all wrapped around her like a memory she'd one day write about.

Mayor Ooglemyer stepped beside her.

"I want you to know," he said quietly, "your book club members, everyone pitching in... your leadership... it saved this place."

"Mayor—"

"No." He shook his head. "For weeks, all I saw was disaster. But then you walked into my office and said we'd figure it out. And now look."

He gestured to the crowd: children sitting on snowbanks drinking cocoa, workers laughing with Poppy, Miss Betty waving pompoms like she was on salary.

Lucy smiled. "We always figure it out."

"That's the problem with this town," he said. "It refuses to stay broken."

As the new foundation settled into place, a flock of ducks landed gently on the pond, waddling to the water's edge as if inspecting the construction site.

Several townsfolk gasped.

"Oh thank God," Lucy's father said, appearing with binoculars. "They're back!"

The ducks quacked approvingly.

Then a family of deer appeared from the tree-line, pausing at the dam's edge.

A murmur rolled through the crowd — soft, amazed, reverent.

Floyd whispered, "Nature has blessed the rebuild. The deer are nodding their approval."

"They're chewing," Michelangelo corrected.

"Same thing," Floyd insisted.

The Bean Hive Rescue and Sanctuary brought back some of the wildlife. Everyone cheered. Slowly, things were moving forward, and in time this will simply be just another ordinary day of happenings with extraordinary memories.

Lucy's phone buzzed.

A text message from her mother, Moira:

"Darling, the ladies from High Tea raised an additional $10,000. Apparently gossip tastes better with charity. Use this for anything the crew needs — equipment, materials, or snacks. Preferably snacks. I was

also able to secure a new investor for the town, who will be investing in marina aquatic life and preservation. I love you"

Lucy laughed out loud.

Poppy peeked over her shoulder.

"Your mom is an icon."

"She is," Lucy admitted, "God help me."

By late afternoon, the last beam was secured. The dam stood strong and straight, reinforced, improved, and shining in the winter sun.

Pete the crew chief handed Lucy a wooden mallet.

"Hello, Mayor Ooglemyer said, you started this whole thing, you will finish it."

Lucy swallowed hard.

The entire town turned toward her.

She lifted the mallet, braced herself, and tapped the final securing peg into place.

A cheer erupted that shook the birch trees.

Poppy burst into full sobs.

Miss Betty yelled, "THE DAM IS SAVED!"

Marvin chanted, "Dam! Dam! Dam!"

Michaelangelo joined, "Dam squad! Dam squad!"

Floyd set off lavender-scented confetti cannons that no one asked for but everyone secretly loved.

Lucy closed her eyes.

She felt Bean Hive breathe again.

Safe.

Stable.

Rebuilt.

Home.

The sun had begun to set in soft layers of peach and pale lavender, streaking across the newly restored dam like a blessing. Workers packed up their tools. Kids tossed snowballs. Steam lifted from cups of hot cocoa as families lingered, unwilling to let the moment end.

Lucy stepped onto the dam, her boots crunching lightly on the packed snow. She ran her fingers along the cool, sturdy beams. Hours before, this had been a symbol of fear — now it was a monument to their stubborn, lovable town.

She looked around.

Poppy was hugging three strangers who had come from the next village over, insisting they take home an extra "Dam Cupcake" because "joy doesn't travel by itself."

Marvin was handing out thermoses of leftover Storm Surge Lattes to the construction crew like he was gifting priceless antiques.

Miss Betty kept patting the dam and declaring to everyone within ten feet:

"Solid! I can FEEL it! This dam will outlive ME!"

Michaelangelo had put up a "You Did It!" glitter banner between two birch trees, though the wind kept twisting it around a branch. Floyd was lecturing a teenager about the proper spiritual alignment of stones, while the teenager nodded politely and clearly understood nothing.

Lucy felt a soft tug on her sleeve.

It was Mayor Ooglemyer.

His eyes were glassy, his bow tie crooked, his nose pink from cold and emotion.

"Lucy," he said quietly, "you saved us."

She shook her head. "No, Mayor... we saved us."

He swallowed hard — the kind of swallow men do when they're trying not to cry in public.

"This village," he said, voice trembling, "this ridiculous, beautiful village... it just—"

He waved a hand in the air, unable to find the words.

Lucy finished for him.

"It refuses to break."

 A tear slipped down the mayor's cheek.

Miss Betty saw it from across the dam and immediately blew her whistle.

"EMOTIONAL EMERGENCY! HUG THE MAYOR!"

 Before he could escape, half a dozen townsfolk surrounded him in a gigantic, warm, slightly suffocating hug. He squeaked like a rubber duck, but his arms slowly lifted, returning the embrace.

 The moment was messy, chaotic, heartfelt — pure Bean Hive Cottage.

 As the crowd quieted, a soft crackling noise echoed

 The soft, rhythmic tapping of water trickling through the new dam.

 Not rushing.

Not spilling wildly.

Just flowing.

Controlled.

Balanced.

Alive.

 The pond, the dam, the village — everything was in harmony again.

 A quiet hush fell over the group. People moved closer, listening.

 Poppy whispered, "It sounds like the town exhaling."

 And Lucy — hand pressed against her chest — felt it too.

 For weeks, tension had sat like a stone in her ribs. And now, standing there among friends, neighbors, and mismatched personalities who somehow made life worth living...

 She felt it lift.

 This was home.

Not because it was perfect.

But because whenever something broke — a dam, a road, a tradition — the people rebuilt it together.

She reached into her coat pocket and pulled out her notebook. On the first clean page she wrote:

"Bean Hive doesn't stay broken.

Not because it never cracks, but because love shows up with a hammer."

She looked up at the dam, the sky, the people she loved.

"News Hot of the Press," she whispered to herself.

A sleek black car pulled up at the edge of Pinehaven Road. Moira stepped out dramatically — faux fur coat, oversized sunglasses, and a thermos she probably didn't fill herself.

She looked around with theatrical pride.

"Well," she announced, "I suppose the crisis is over, the wildlife is safe, and my daughter is once again underappreciated."

Poppy yelled from the cocoa table, "Moira! You made it!"

Moira approached Lucy, cupping her daughter's cheeks.

"You did it, darling," she said softly. "I couldn't be prouder."

Lucy blinked back tears.

"Mom... Thank you. For the fundraiser, for the check, for—"

Moira waved it off. "Nonsense. Saving quaint New England-esque East Coast Long Island villages is practically a hobby."

Everyone gathered for a group photo on the rebuilt dam — Mayor Ooglemyer in the center, Miss Betty holding her sign, Poppy raising a cupcake triumphantly, Floyd misting everyone with "Celebratory Bergamot Mist," Marvin lifting his coffee cup, Moira stepping in at the last second to adjust the angle because "lighting matters."

Lucy stood in the front, notebook in hand.

Michelangelo counted down.

"Three... two... one..."

The camera flashed just as the first star appeared in the winter sky.

And in that moment — surrounded by laughter, love, cold noses, warm hearts, and a restored dam humming beneath their feet —

Lucy knew this wasn't just the end of a chapter.

It was the beginning of something much bigger.

Something she would write about.

Something she would remember forever.

Something Bean Hive Cottage, her book clubs, would one day tell stories about in the diner, at the bakery, in the apothecary, and at town hall meetings for years.

The Great Dam Crisis.

The storm that tried.

The village that refused to break.

And the girl who helped save it.

Montauk Mystery with Bean Hive Cottage

BEAN HIVE COTTAGE SERIES MYSTERY-THE LETTER IN THE WALL

The Letter in the Wall

Most nights in Bean Hive Cottage ended quietly.

A lamp left glowing.

A kettle cooling on the stove.

Footsteps softened as the inn settled into its familiar creaks and sighs.

Tonight was not one of those nights.

Lucy stood alone in the hallway where the wallpaper had peeled away earlier. The newly exposed section of plaster still held traces of dust and old glue—evidence of something hidden, something forgotten. And on the table beside her sat the bottle they had found.

Strange how a single object could feel like the beginning of everything.

She lifted the bottle gently. Even empty now, it carried the weight of the letter within it—the faded ink, the lighthouse sketch, the date from decades ago. The message itself had been heartbreakingly brief, but powerful enough that Lucy felt it echoing through her chest even now.

If this reaches you...

Meet me where the water meets the sky. At The End.

At the light.

— M.

Montauk.

It had to be Montauk. Montauk on Long Island, was always known as "The End."

But why hide something like this inside her wall?

Why seal a message meant for someone else and bury it inside a cottage miles away from somewhere?

And who was "M"?

The aftertaste of the unknown lingered like a whisper. Lucy could sense it—this wasn't a random discovery. Someone had placed the bottle there with intention. Someone who knew the cottage decades ago. Someone who wanted their words to survive even if they couldn't. What was the story behind this? Who sent the letter, where did this all begin? Who was "M" meeting?

Lucy set the bottle down and opened the letter again.

A torn scrap she hadn't noticed earlier slid out from behind it, fluttering onto the table like a final breath.

Three faded words stared back at her:

Find the first.

The first What?

The first Clue?

The first Letter?

The first Lighthouse?

The first... Person?

Lucy pressed her palm against her forehead.

This wasn't a mystery tucked into the past.

This was a path—one she had already stepped onto without meaning to.

She folded the letter carefully and placed it back into the bottle's wrappings.

Whatever the letter meant...

whatever the storm of 1978 had taken...

whatever truth had been hidden inside her wall for decades...

Someone had left a trail.

And the first breadcrumb had finally been found.

As Lucy turned out the hallway light, she glanced over her shoulder at the exposed plaster one last time.

Tomorrow, she would search again.

She wasn't sure for what.

But she could feel it:

This was only the beginning.

Stay tuned the next series book will reveal more about this Bean Hive Cottage Mystery.

From the author

A MESSAGE FROM LUCILLE

Thank you for stepping into Bean Hive Cottage with me.

This world is built from the small, magical pieces of Long Island—sunshine, stormy nights, salty air, hidden histories, and the quiet secrets tucked into old walls.

The mystery you discovered in this book is only the beginning.

The Montauk letter has more to say, and Book Two continues the search one clue at a time. We will embark on not just the story of Bean Hive Cottage tales, but the mystery inspired by each book in the series.

Thank you for reading.

I can't wait to bring you deeper into the mystery.

Cheers,

Lucille Huckelbarel

www.ingramcontent.com/pod-product-compliance
Lightning Source LLC
Chambersburg PA
CBHW031053310726
48969CB00007B/2255